Bunwych

The Enchanted Village

by
Jon Fabris

interior illustrations by

Jon Fabris

Cover Illustration by Jamie Noble Frier, The Noble Artist

JAF Productions
Copyright © 2018, 2022 Jon Fabris
All rights reserved.

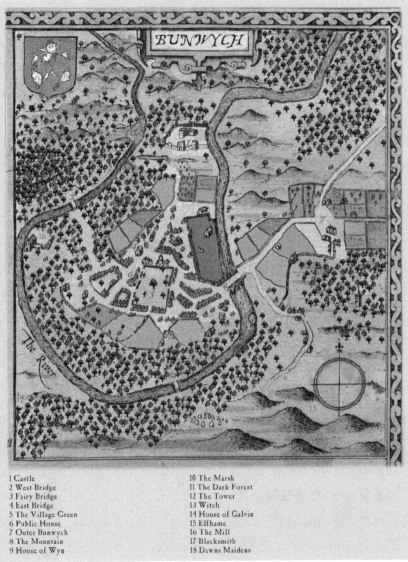

1 Castle	10 The Marsh
2 West Bridge	11 The Dark Forest
3 Fairy Bridge	12 The Tower
4 East Bridge	13 Witch
5 The Village Green	14 House of Galvin
6 Public House	15 Elfhame
7 Outer Bunwych	16 The Mill
8 The Mountain	17 Blacksmith
9 House of Wyn	18 Dawns Maidens

Table of Contents

Prologue 9
    The Trial 11
    The Changeling 18
Six Months Before Midsummer's Eve 25
    The Troll Princess 25
Three Months Before Midsummer's Eve 33
    Mung the Ogre 33
One Month Before Midsummer's Eve 35
    Prince Terrell 35
    The Dwarf Bride 38
    The Changeling 46
Two Weeks Before Midsummer's Eve 47
    The First Impossible Task 47
    Midsummer Festival 49
    The Wild Man 52
Four Days Before Midsummer's Eve 59
    The Goblin Servant 59
    Terrell's Expedition 63
    The Second Impossible Task 65
    Terrell Is Captured 67
    The Swan Faerie 74
    The Witch 79
    The Dwarf King Returns a Hero 83
    Terrell Arrives 86

- Three Days Before Midsummer's Eve ... 97
  - Witches' Revenge ... 100
  - Terrell's Second Night – The Phantom Hound ... 102
- Two Days Before Midsummer's Eve ... 103
  - The Blacksmith ... 103
  - Terrell's Third Night – The Spectral King ... 106
- One Day Before Midsummer's Eve ... 111
  - The Promise ... 112
  - Morris Flies A Broom ... 116
  - The Third Task – Chop Down a Tree With Water ... 121
  - The False Bride ... 125
  - Terrell's Fourth Night – The Ghostly Queen ... 128
- Midsummer's Eve (day) ... 131
- Midsummer's Eve (night) ... 135
  - The Faerie Ball ... 135
  - Terrell's Fifth Night - The Ball, Troll Attack ... 150
  - Confessions ... 153
- Midsummer's Day ... 155
  - Confessions – The Curse ... 157
  - Wyn's Revenge ... 159
  - Terrell's Sixth Night - Funeral ... 163
- Two Days After Midsummer's Eve ... 165
  - The Second Wedding ... 165
  - Terrell Helps Galvin ... 168
  - Morris Meets His Father ... 176
- Three Days After Midsummer's Day ... 179

Alec's Quest..193
    The Dragon Quest..201
Visit to the Past..218
Samhain...249
Samhain Night...252
Yule..259
Beltaine..260

Prologue

Once upon a time, in a certain kingdom there was a village called Bunwych. This village was very special, not because of its great wealth, or spectacular architecture, or famous citizens, but due to its extraordinary location. It was situated in a river valley just next to an ancient group of standing stones called the Dawns Maidens. Although faerie-land (or Elfhame as it is called by its inhabitants), exists in a separate world from ours, there are connections between our world and theirs. Bunwych is one such connection.

Creatures that were rare or never seen in the rest of the Kingdom, such as elves, giants, trolls, dwarfs, or goblins, although not a frequent sight, were not uncommon in Bunwych. Talking rabbits, mysterious towers appearing and disappearing, walking trees, bottomless satchels, water running uphill, flying wheel barrels, harps which play themselves, giant turnips, singing tulips, are all considered natural phenomena in Bunwych.

The people in this community were for the most part very close and they mistrusted strangers. Visitors inquiring if they have reached Bunwych are likely to meet with a friendly Bunwychian smiling and pointing in the opposite direction. Indeed, the very trees, air, and soil seem to conspire together to protect the town. Travelers passing through the town experience strange and sometimes troubling occurrences. Although, after they leave the town limits they often forget, or rationalize the experience as something mundane.

There is a ruined castle of modest size north of the village which has long since been abandoned and is rumored to be haunted. The village has no lord, and the little government that is necessary is made up of a group of town elders. The kingdom of course has a king, but tiny Bunwych is not on any maps, and whether it be through magic or cunning the villagers have managed to keep the tax collectors away.

The Trial

Three children sat solemnly in a clearing, as if waiting for something to begin. Alec, the oldest, was fifteen. Next was Julia, thirteen. They each sat on a large, round stone, fuzzy with moss. Before them, on a long, moss covered log, was Nessa, who was five. The glade was surrounded by majestic trees which kept the small clearing in deep shade.

Another child arrived, Morris, who was nine. He took his seat on the log next to his sister Nessa and now there were four.

"You're late Morris," said Alec.

"Melinda was stuck in a bramble and I had to free her," Morris replied.

Alec ignored this and began the proceedings. "I have gathered us here today to give trial. I will be prosecutor, Julia will be defender, and you two shall be the jury and decide the fate of the accused."

Morris raised his hand, "Who are the accused?"

"The accused is our mother, and her crimes are many. First, she has lied to us for our entire lives. Secondly, and worse, she is, as I have long suspected, not a simple country woman, but a faerie." Alec said this last word with dramatic effect. Nessa was struck dumb, her mouth hanging open wide. The effect on Morris was different. He started laughing.

Julia spoke, "You're being silly Alec. Our mother is not a faerie."

"It is true and I have proof. Remember last summer when there was drought and all the cows in the village went dry? Well ours didn't, and it was due to faerie magic."

"We just had a deeper well than most," Julia retorted.

"Second, there is no iron in the house, not a morsel."

"So?" Julia said.

"Iron is the bane of faeries. They hate it."

"We have pewter spoons and knives. They're better," Julia said.

"Last fall Nessa lost a tooth. She put the tooth under her pillow as is our custom. I endeavored to stay awake that night to witness the faerie's visit. At midnight I saw the faerie come in and swap the tooth for a penny. It was our mother."

"Our mother isn't the tooth faerie you stupid donkey," Julia said.

Nessa giggled.

Alec ignored her and continued, "My most important evidence I found just yesterday. I was watching our mother through a chink in the wall. She was cooking scones and left them too long. When she took them out they were burnt to a crisp. I saw them and smelled the smoke! She looked about, and when she thought no one was watching, she pulled the scones out of the oven and they were perfect, golden brown."

"You smelled the crumbs that fell to the bottom of the oven and burned," Julia said.

"It is true my siblings. Our mother is a faerie. And I think our father is not away fighting a war as she always tells us. He is probably in Elfhame imprisoned or enchanted. And her worst crime is keeping from us our rightful inheritance. For if we are faeries, we should be living in a palace in the Other-world with fine silk clothing and furniture of gold."

"Nonsense. Don't listen to our brother. He reads too many tales. Mother wouldn't lie to us." (who is talking here?)

"Well, jury, what do you say? Are we faeries or regular mortals?"

Nessa smiled and said enthusiastically, "Faeries!" Truth be told, Nessa looked upon her older brother as a kind of god and would have accepted that they were whales if Alec had wished her to think so.

Morris, however, always played the rival to his older and only brother. He looked at Alec defiantly and said, "Not faeries!"

Julia, with smug satisfaction, said, "There, votes must be unanimous to convict, so she is innocent."

Alec stared back at Morris with smoldering gravity for a moment then said, "Very well. But I will find more evidence, and you will soon know the truth. In the meantime tell no one of this. Got that Nessa?"

Nessa covered her mouth with one hand and lifted the other in oath.

"Morris?" Alec said.

Morris reluctantly gave his oath and the trial was adjourned.

Alec lay on the river bank thinking about his mother.

He remembered a time long ago when she broke down sobbing on the bare floor of their cottage after burning a meal. He asked what was wrong and she said "Mommy just misses home." He quickly pushed this thought away, not liking how it made him feel.

He had always felt she harbored some secret. Sometimes he would spy on her when she thought she was alone. She would stare off into the horizon with a slight smile on her face as if remembering past times. Other times she seemed mysterious, like she was an agent of some secret plan and not necessarily a benevolent one. Yet, other times she seemed like some powerful goddess, temporarily banished to earth for some godly transgression. These times he feared her. Not because she would do him harm or didn't love him, that was never in question, but because of sheer, awesome power, like that one feels when watching mighty waves batter an ocean cliff.

Her mortal skills, however, were somewhat lacking. The house was never particularly clean nor were the children. Meals often burned or were simply inedible. Unlike most of the village women she couldn't spin or sew and depended on barter with the other villagers for clothing.

She was good with livestock, however, and seemed to have a rapport with them and all other animals. Once, a poisonous snake had crept into the childrens sleeping attic. She calmly told the kids to wait downstairs while she climbed the ladder to the attic. A few moments later she returned, cradling the snake gently in her arms and set it loose again outside.

She didn't associate much with others in the village but sometimes would ask a neighbor to watch the children for the night. Sometimes she would leave for several days at a time. Where she went and what she did in these times he didn't know.

One day several years ago when Alec was six and Nessa was a newborn, Wyn made arrangements with a neighbor named Radella to watch her babies for the night. Wyn had on her finest dress and primped in front of the mirror. There came a rap on the door and she jumped, startled. She opened the door and Radella stood there, smiling.

"They have all been fed. They should sleep soundly all night," she said as she walked back to the cupboard and took out a tiny bottle. She noticed Radella was still in the doorway and said to her, "Please Radella, come in."

Wyn handed her the bottle and said, "Julia has a little cough, if she wakes up give her a little of this."

"Don't worry Wyn. The children are safe with me."

Wyn rushed out the door, excited about the evening. When she reached the crossroads between her house and the main road she suddenly froze, her eyes wide with terror. Radella did not enter immediately as she normally would, and only entered when invited in. When the cottage was built, she herself had cast a powerful spell of warding on it preventing any monster, beast, or faerie being from entering unless invited in. In a panic, she turned and raced back to the house.

Wyn

As she reached the threshold of the cottage, the door and window shutters burst open, and she flew inside, the air crackling with energy. Her hair billowed out as if she were in a gale. Inside the house was a gruesome troll, the enchantment that made it appear as Radella now dispelled. It was hunched over to fit under the low ceiling of the cottage, and was clutching a large burlap sack which contained four squirming children.

Wyn's semblance of an ordinary human woman was also gone, and there stood the daughter of a faerie Queen; wild, awesome, and terrible. Her countenance was so fierce that the troll stood frozen to the spot, terrified. She waved her hands and a flash of light burst forth, for an instant as bright as the sun. The flesh of the troll crackled and turned to stone in a matter of seconds. With the danger averted, she once again appeared like an ordinary human woman who feared for her children and she rushed over to the sack. She pulled them out one by one, examined them for any wounds, and finding none, hugged each one tightly.

This was not the first or last attempt by the faerie queen to steal her children, for Wynn knew she was involved. She strengthened the protective charms around the cottage, and planted rowan trees around the house, even though it weakened her own power.

The Changeling

Millard was a poor farmer who lived in outer Bunwych. He had a small plot of land. The soil was heavy clay and it wasn't very productive. He and his wife Bess had two young daughters and despite their hard work, they seldom had enough to eat.

One day he was tending his meager garden when he saw a rabbit nibbling at some greens. He took out his bow and shot at the rabbit but missed. It ran off into the forest. He gave chase, determined to catch the thief and provide the family with some meat for supper. For hours he chased the rabbit, always just behind but just as he was about to draw back the bow for a shot, the rabbit would dash away.

He found himself in a part of the forest he had never been before. The trees were ancient and massive and there were scaly, wooden towers that looked as though they would almost touch the sun. Suddenly, in the clearing, there appeared a splendid palace, built of shining white marble. Amazed, he went inside.

There were a hundred elves, all seated at a great long table. They were laughing and celebrating and having a splendid feast. There was venison, pork, rabbit, all manner of fruits, bread of all shapes and varieties, wine, both red and white, beer, and mead. A beautiful lady smiled and motioned for him to join them. She had a long, graceful neck and though she had long, white hair, she looked quite young. He hadn't eaten since the day before and could not resist the offer.

He sat down and began ravenously eating and drinking. The people were very friendly and laughed and jested with him, especially the woman with the white hair, who he soon learned was the queen. The party lasted many hours until his belly was full and he was quite drunk.

"I wish I could eat like this every day," Millard said.

The queen replied, "Then why don't you?"

"I am a poor man. I have a plot of land but no matter how hard I work, I pull nothing out of the ground but a few stunted turnips," he said.

"I will bless your land and give you all that you wish. And when you have your first boy you will send him here and he will live with us in our palace."

Millard was tempted by the offer, and although he would have to give up his first boy, he would get to live here in splendor like a prince. But then he thought of his wife.

"I am grateful, Your Highness, but my wife will be grieved to lose one of her babies," he said.

"Fear not, we will send one of our children to take his place. She never needs to know," she said.

Foolishly, Millard agreed and the queen produced a piece of parchment and a pen and ink. It had writing on it but Millard could not read. Nevertheless, he took the pen and signed the spot she pointed to with his mark.

All of a sudden the room seemed to change. The people began to leave and the laughing and joking turned to tense silence.

"You may leave now," the queen said coldly.

He staggered out of the door and into the bright sunlight. He turned back to look but the splendid palace had disappeared, in its place was an empty field.

When he returned home, he realized four days had passed. Bess, his wife, was worried but he told her only that he was lost in the forest and could not find his way home until now.

As the queen had promised, his land soon became productive and his family had plenty to eat. A year passed and his wife had another child, a son. Millard remembered the bargain he had made with the queen of the elves and was worried. He sat by his son's crib every night, never moving from his sight.

The months passed and his baby seemed happy and normal, and he began to think the queen had forgotten the bargain, or was jesting.

As a matter of fact, the queen had remembered, and the very night the baby was born, she swapped him with a goblin newborn and cast a spell on him to make him look human. The real boy, who was named Liam, lived not in the palace with the queen as she promised, but in a filthy hovel in Elfhame with a goblin family. He had two step sisters who were wicked and hated the human boy.

The false Liam also had two step sisters, named Elinor and Kyla. They loved their brother and doted on him although he was usually colicky and cried often.

She led him just out of the goblin village to an enormous tree. At first, he couldn't see the way into her home, but then she stepped into a crevasse between two roots.

The real Liam did not fare so well. He lived in a dirty hut amongst many others, crowded in the goblin village deep in the forest. His step parents made him do all of the housework and he was rarely allowed to leave the family hut. He had two step sisters who were wicked and hated the human boy. They played tricks on him, telling him he was a freak. He knew he looked different than all the other goblin children, and felt like an outcast. Occasionally his sisters and sometimes his step parents would call him "human" in anger, but having never seen another human, he assumed it was a general insult. Only occasionally would he see an elf in passing, and then only adults, but he could never imagine he was one of such a graceful race as they.

One day when he was seven, Liam was fetching water from the well in the center of the goblin village when he saw an elderly elf woman at the well. She was very old and feeble and was having trouble raising the bucket out of the well.

"Please, can I help you?" Liam said.

The ancient elf paused in her lifting of the bucket and squinted down at the young boy.

"Why thank you."

Liam raised up the bucket and carefully poured the water into the pail she had on the ground, not spilling a drop. When he was finished he looked up at the little elf and offered, "Please, may I help you carry the bucket?"

"Yes, that would be lovely."

He picked up the bucket and followed the old faerie. She led him just out of the goblin village to an enormous tree. At first, he couldn't see the way into her home, but then she stepped into a crevasse between two roots. He hesitated.

"Come in," she encouraged.

He went inside and found himself in a lovely round room that was not at all damp or gloomy, and much bigger than the tree looked. She told him to sit and served him tea and biscuits. They talked for hours about nothing in particular.

He learned that her name was Maeraddyth Winterflower. She was so ancient that neither she nor anyone else could remember how old she was. For reasons no one knew, she was shunned by her fellow elves and lived in a mean part of the forest, near the goblins.

When he returned home, he was late and his step parents beat him, but that didn't snuff the joy he felt inside. Despite the beating, Liam returned to visit Maeraddyth nearly every day. She would feed him badly needed food and in return, he joyfully did little chores for her. She also began educating him, teaching him to read and about the outside world which was up to now a complete mystery to him. In time, she began to teach him magic. He was very clever and learned quickly.

Liam's life was grim but he lived for the hour or two when he could get away to the tree. Something in him knew that his destiny was not to perish in a goblin hovel, and he persevered and kept his spirits high.

After a few months, Liam came to her with a swollen eye from being hit by his goblin father. She told him to bring her to them. He waited outside while she went in. Liam heard his goblin father arguing with her, followed by a sharp snapping sound and a cry of pain. Maeraddyth walked out with a demure smile on her face and told Liam that she had made a bargain with the goblins and he would from then on be living with her. This made him very happy.

Then, one day, the midsummer day of his eighth year, she put a drop of a potion into his tea. When he had taken three sips he fell into a deep, peaceful sleep. She covered him with a blanket, wrote a short note, placing it atop a large book, and left, never to return.

Liam didn't wake until the next morning. He felt refreshed and no worse for the wear but confused. Maeraddyth was gone.

He saw the note. It read *Liam, read this.*

He opened the book to the first page. At first it was blank but as he watched, writing appeared as if she were writing it at that moment.

Liam, I am sorry but I had to go away. But I will still be with you. Read this book. Every day there will be a new lesson from me. Yours truly, Maeraddyth Winterflower.

As she promised, every day when Liam came and opened the book, a new page would be written, sometimes with a drawing. The lessons progressed in difficulty as he grew older and he began to learn some powerful magic.

Meanwhile, back in Bunwych, Millard sometimes suspected his son was not really his, but pushed these uncomfortable thoughts to the back of his mind. He was prospering and was by now one of the richest men in Bunwych.

One fine spring day Bess was washing clothes down by the river with her daughters. Liam, now five, was playing in the river, trying to catch fish with a small net. Suddenly Elinor screamed. Liam was sitting on the riverbank. He had just bitten the head off of a small fish he had caught. He turned to Elinor and smiled as he chomped away at the raw fish. Bess yelled at him to drop the fish but he turned from her, hunched over, and continued eating. She had a wet towel and began hitting him with it, shouting, "Throw that filthy thing away!" Finally he did, and ran off back to the house.

There was another disturbing incident a year or so later. Elinor had gone to the well to draw some water. When the pail came up out of the well she screamed. There were two dead kittens, drowned. The same kittens she had seen her brother playing with in the barn that day. He denied having anything to do with the drowning and even denied playing with them that day.

Six Months Before Midsummer's Eve

The Troll Princess

It was a cold winter night. The wind howled outside but the shutters were tight and held its frosty enemy at the gate. It was bedtime and the children were huddled under thick blankets, with only their faces visible. Alec and Morris were in one bed, and Julia and Nessa were in the other. Their mother, Wyn was between them sitting on a stool.

With no book to read from, she began a story.

"Once upon a time there lived a king, a queen, and their young daughter named Eloise. This princess was so beautiful that the queen of the elves was jealous of her. One night the faerie queen sent her goblin henchmen to Eloise's bedroom to steal her away. Luckily the king came into her bedroom to say goodnight just as the evil goblins appeared in her window. He was a strong warrior and managed to fight them off. He called for his guards and they pursued the fiends with hounds but they managed to escape.

The very next day the king summoned his wisest councilors and asked them how to protect his beloved daughter. The plan they forged was this; the most powerful magician in the kingdom would be hired to cast a powerful spell of protection on the castle. She would be safe as long as she was within its walls. From that day forward the princess was to never leave the castle grounds.

Years passed and Eloise grew even more beautiful and the queen of the elves even more jealous. The princess

There, in a clearing was a bed made of stone. A beautiful young elf lay there. Her eyes were closed and she was as pale as parchment. By her side looking very grave was another elf, very beautiful with a crown of gold.

was kept safe by the protection of the spell and the king's guards. Memories of the kidnapping incident faded and the princess began to roam further and the guards grew less vigilant.

The queen bided her time and one day the princess was alone in a meadow just past the castle walls picking flowers. There, the protection of the spell was weakened, but yet still too strong for anything bad to befall.

A pretty little pixie appeared a few yards away, just on the edge of the great woods. She called to the princess, "Please, I have been summoned by the queen of the elves to fetch you. Our young princess lies dying and only the touch of a human princess can save her. Will you come with me? I promise no evil will befall you."

The princess was as kind as she was beautiful and her heart bled at the words of the pixie. For just a moment she hesitated, then followed.

She stepped past the meadow into the great forest. The way soon became gloomy and the air grew still. The pixie led her along a path into a grove of mighty trees. There, in a clearing was a bed made of stone. A beautiful young elf lay there. Her eyes were closed and she was as pale as parchment.

By her side looking very grave was another elf, very beautiful with a crown of gold.

Eloise bowed to the queen.

The queen smiled and took her hand, "We are grateful you have come."

"What am I to do?" Eloise asked.

"Just a drop of your blood will revive her." The queen then produced a long, sharp needle.

Eloise was frightened when she saw the needle, but just then the elven princess moaned and stirred a little and her heart was moved. Bravely she held out her hand to the queen.

The queen smiled, then pricked her with the long needle. All at once the princess was transformed into a horrible, ugly troll. The queen laughed cruelly and the sick elven princess, who was only acting sick, opened her eyes, sat up, and laughed. Then, without a word, the queen and her false daughter disappeared, leaving the transformed Eloise alone deep in the great woods.

Eloise tried to find her way home but was hopelessly lost. At last she found a trail and followed it to a small town. She emerged from the woods nearby a small crowd of people. She tried to ask them for help but the sounds that came out of her mouth were frightening troll bellows. The people screamed and ran. In a moment several men appeared armed with pitchforks and spears. Eloise was frightened and ran for her life. She just barely managed to escape the men hunting her.

In despair, Eloise wandered the forest all night until she came upon an abandoned hunters cabin. There she lived for years, always careful to avoid all humans. Her only friends were the birds and small creatures of the forest who, somehow, were still able to see her as she really was. One day she chanced to find a small mirror that had been lost in the woods. She looked into it, expecting to see a hideous troll, instead, she saw her true self, unchanged from the day when she first was bewitched. She kept the mirror hanging above her bed in the little cabin and gazed into it every day.

Then, one day, a young prince was out hunting and came into the town. He heard from the townspeople of a horrible monster that was occasionally seen in the great woods. He resolved to go and slay this beast.

For many days he searched the forest, until at last he found a trail which led to an old cabin. He drew his sword and went inside. Eloise was there sleeping but the prince only saw a horrible troll. He was about to plunge his sword into the troll when he glanced at the mirror above the bed. There he saw not a troll, but a young lady, the most beautiful girl he had ever seen. Eloise awoke and was terrified when she saw the boy in her room with a sword.

"Please don't hurt me," she cried.

While looking through the mirror the prince could see her lips move and understand her. He lowered his sword and asked her how she came to be this way.

She told him how she was tricked and bewitched by the queen of the elves and how she had lived here alone in the forest for so many years. They sat talking for a long time, and the prince's love for Eloise grew. Morning came, and the prince closed his eyes and kissed her. Instantly she transformed back into a princess, exactly as she was when first bewitched, she was not even aged a day. The couple's happiness was beyond measure, and the prince took Eloise back to his castle where they planned to wed the next day.

They had just arrived in the castle when the sun set, and as the last dying rays flickered off, the princess instantly became a hideous troll again. And so it continued. By day, Eloise was a beautiful princess, but at night she inevitably transformed back into a troll. The couple was wed and they were very happy, but the princess had to hide in her chambers at night so that no one in the kingdom would know of her terrible curse. They lived happily for many years and had two normal children but the prince was discontent. He longed to have his wife normal at night time and be able to take her to evening balls. One day, without telling Eloise. The prince embarked on a quest to find the faerie queen and beg her to lift the curse.

After many weeks of searching he found her, and was able to obtain an audience with her. He begged her most humbly and sweetly, but her heart was of stone, and instead of lifting the curse, the queen redoubled it. She cast the prince out of her court, saying he was lucky to be let live.

The prince returned to his castle only to find his wife gone. She left him a note.

It read:

> *My dear husband, I begged you to be content and not seek out the faerie queen. Now the curse has been burgeoned and I am a dragon, by night and by day. I must fly far away and cloister myself far away from humankind. Remember always that I love you and our dear ones.*

The prince was beside himself with grief but the very next day he embarked on a journey to find his wife. For seven long years he searched, chasing any scant rumor or sighting of dragons. Then one day he arrived on a lonely island far to the north where a dragon was said to lair. Bravely, he walked into an ice cave unarmed, ready to either meet his beloved or die. The dragon woke from its slumber and stood, staring down at the man. He looked at her through the small mirror he held and saw..."

Here Wyn paused and looked at her girls to the right and the boys to the left. They were all staring at her in wait, even Alec.

"Momma, what did he see?" Nessa exclaimed.

"He saw his dearest wife."

Wyn became still and blinked several times, staring off into space.

"What happened next Momma?" Nessa asked.

"The prince kissed her and she was human again, and would remain so to the end of their long happy days."

Quickly, Wyn got up and went to Nessa, kissed her, and patted Julia's head.

"Goodnight my dear ones," she said and blew out the lamp and climbed back down the ladder to the lower floor.

"Why does Momma cry like that when she tells us stories?" Nessa asked.

Alec said, "Because she's a silly female."

"You hush! It's because she misses our father," Julia said.

"What was father like Alec?" Nessa asked.

"I don't remember," Alec answered sullenly, which was true. All he remembered was a tall man with dark hair. His face was only a blur.

Mung the Ogre

Three Months Before Midsummer's Eve

Mung the Ogre

There was an ogre named Mung which lived in a small valley north of the Dark Forest who was so old he could barely see. This ogre's marauding days were long behind him and he contented himself with tending a small flock of sheep, living off the milk and meat of his animals. This did not matter to the village boys who knew only that he was a monster, and therefore, an enemy. A favorite sport of the village boys was to visit this pitiable monster and molest him from atop a cliff where they would be safe from his wrath. On this day the expedition was Alec, Kerwin the Miller's son, and Nolan, the son of the cattle farmer. This boy, being a year older, and much bigger and stronger than the other boys, gave the others more courage.

After a long paddle up the river they pulled their makeshift raft up a gentle bank and began the walk up the mountain. The forest was quiet and dark as they climbed their way up the steep, rocky slope. At last they reached the apex and they beheld the valley below. There were giant trees and patches of rough pasture where the ogre led his sheep.

The ogre was nowhere in sight but soon they heard distant bells, which could only mean that the ogre's sheep, and therefore, the ogre, were approaching. He appeared over a hill, his back stooped and his head containing only a few threads of gray hair. The boys wasted no time and began shouting out vulgar but hilarious (to them) obscenities to the ogre. The ogre raised his head and looked about but couldn't see the source of the abuse. He walked towards the sound and finally spotted the boys up along the cliff, too far for him to reach. He shouted out in rage and shook his crook at the boys.

This continued for a time until Mung began to ignore them

and fun began to wear off. It was Alec who threw the first rock. It hit Mung in the back and he swung around at the boys and bellowed at them. They all picked up rocks and began raining missiles down at the ogre. Alec, wanting to show off, picked up a rock the size of his fist, and hit the ogre square between the eyes. Mung was infuriated. Blood trickled from his wound. He ran at the cliff, swinging his crook at the boys. Surprised by his quickness, the boys had to back off up the steep cliff. Nolan tripped on some loose rocks, stumbled, and seemingly in slow motion as the other two watched in horror, slid down the slope, disappearing over the cliff.

Mung stopped his attack and bent down to the boy. The others rushed back to the cliff edge and looked down, horrified. Nolan was splayed on the grass, unconscious. The ogre picked him up and ate him in seven bites.

Not a word was spoken on the long voyage home. Too shocked to comprehend the finality of what had happened, their main fear was the punishment that would inevitably come.

Kerwin's father beat him, but Alec was not punished. Wyn merely looked at him sadly, knowing the guilt he already felt was punishment enough.

One Month Before Midsummer's Eve

Prince Terrell

A chipmunk stood on a rock and nibbled a seed he found on the forest floor. Just then he cocked his head, uttered a chirp of alarm, and disappeared under a tree root.

Prince Terrell and his ten men were crashing through the forest on foot, making as much noise as an army of elephants. They had traveled for several weeks all the way from the king's castle and were tired, scratched, and forlorn.

Terrell was the youngest of the king's six children, and the fourth boy in line for the throne. As a lad he was feckless and careless, but in the last seven years while he was under the stewardship of his uncle, he had grown into a fine young man, training him in the arts of war, and the softer principles of chivalry. He just returned to court and was determined to succeed in this his first task from the king. For the king's ongoing and endless war a stronghold was needed in a particular strategic location. An old man in the court remembered there was once a castle in this region, in a town called Bunwych. Terrell was commanded to go there and determine if the castle would make a suitable garrison for the king's army.

The road to Bunwych was very hard to find for someone who had never been there, and so they were forced to hack their way through the dense forest. The branches of the trees seemed to bend into their way as they passed. Thorns and stinging nettles grew in abundance. Countless times they followed a path which seemed clear and then suddenly they would find themselves funneled into a hollow surrounded on three sides by a tangle of fallen trees and branches so dense that they were forced to double back on their path and start again. On their third night the horses were spooked and somehow became loose and ran off.

When the men started grumbling under their breaths and glaring at him behind his back, he gave stern orders and showed no sign of weakening, although he was worried about the situation because they were running low on food. At last they reached a bubbling stream and Terrell knew that following the stream would lead them to the river which would then lead them to Bunwych.

Evening was approaching and soon they would need to make camp. One of the men at the rear spotted a plump doe, very close, just standing there watching him. He quickly pulled out his bow and took aim. Just as he was about to fire, it darted off. Not wanting to lose the opportunity for his first taste of meat in weeks, he followed. Unfortunately for him, the deer was enchanted, and he would never catch it nor would he be able to break off the chase until he was dead with exhaustion. Later, when they broke for camp, Terrell noticed his group was one man short and assumed the man had deserted. In the middle of the night one of the men woken up and looked up to see a beautiful maiden, scantily clad, beckoning him to follow. As he followed her a path seemed to open up to him as he passed. She disappeared through a thick wall of leaves. He followed and fell to his death into a deep ravine.

The following morning Terrell woke to find another man missing. Thinking he deserted, he warned his men if anyone else tried to desert him they would meet the end of his sword. The man was not the only thing missing, however. The evening before they had camped within sight of a wide stream but now the stream was gone. The men grumbled about sorcery.

Terrell was alarmed but didn't let the men see that. Estimating the direction they were traveling yesterday, he led the troops on. They soon passed a distinctive tree; an oak that had been struck by lightning and grew into an odd bow shape. The men trudged wearily along all day, many times having to deviate from a straight path due to thick brambles and underbrush. Towards dusk the party stopped to prepare camp when one of the men looked up with horror and pointed. There in front of them was the bow shaped oak, the very one they had passed ten hours earlier.

The Dwarf Bride

Deep in the heart of the salt mines that wound their way far beneath Bunwych lived the dwarf King Gomrund. He was a widower but the customary 33 years of mourning had recently passed and he was now courting a fair dwarf maiden.

One day he was sitting on his throne which was carved out of a single block of salt crystal. His betrothed was on his knee, and he asked her how much she loved him.

She answered, "I love you like faeries love flowers."

This was not a wise thing to say, for the only thing the king hated more than flowers was faeries. Without hesitation the king took up his ax and beheaded her with one fell blow.

After a moment of reflection, Gomrund was ashamed at his behavior.

"I will not wed a dwarf," he proclaimed, partly as atonement for his action, and partly because he was sick of dwarf females and their strange ways.

He asked his wise man and chief adviser, "Who is the fairest of all the human maidens?"

Arngrim replied, "The fairest maiden is named Lyneth and dwells in the village above us."

The dwarf king decided to venture out into the overground and see the girl for himself. He put on his finest cloak and emerged with Arngrim into the sunlight, blinking in the unaccustomed brightness.

Lyneth was there, in a dirty work frock, her golden hair a wild mess.

Gomrund said, "You must invent some kind of device that shields the eyes from the nasty sunlight."

"Brilliant idea Your Eminence. I will put a committee on it forthwith," his adviser said.

They walked only a short while then stopped and peered out under a hedge into a field of crops. Lyneth was there, in a dirty work frock, her golden hair a wild mess. She was bending over a turnip and pulling mightily.

"She is there," Arngrim said.

"What, behind that filthy peasant in the field?" the king said, craning his neck to see around her.

"No Your Eminence, that is she," Arngrim answered patiently.

Suddenly the turnip gave way and she fell backwards, particles of dirt flying into her face and hair.

"Are you sure?" Gomrund asked incredulously.

"Yes, Your Eminence."

"Not very promising but as long as I am here," the king said as he slipped through the hedge. The aged adviser followed, doing his best to preserve his dignity.

Lyneth didn't hear them approach and bent over to have at another turnip. The king stood there behind her and cleared his throat. She didn't hear him. This was an unaccustomed situation for the king. He felt embarrassed then remembered that he was the king of all the dwarfs and became angry and pinched her bottom.

Lyneth screamed, turned around and slapped the king so hard that he fell back over a turnip hill. Arngrim was shocked and couldn't move, striking the king was a capital offense.

Lyneth could only stare, she had never seen a dwarf before and was certainly not expecting two of them to be lurking behind her in the field.

Gomrund started laughing. Never had a dwarf female showed such spirit in front of him. He was smitten.

"You will love the Under Kingdom my dear. The walls sparkle with a million precious gems and the air is redolent with mushrooms and damp, rich earth. I will leave my adviser to work out the details. I shall return in one week."

The king bowed low, then strode off at a happy swagger. Lyneth stared at him uncomprehending.

Arngrim took out a scroll, "Just a few formalities, do you have any Elfin blood?"

She blinked and furrowed her eyebrows.

"No? Good."

She turned and ran off. He tried to follow, but was much slower than the girl. "Now, the matter of the dowry, a customary sum would be twenty pounds of gold-"

"Very well, we will return tomorrow with the dowry!" he shouted after her.

Lyneth was a simple girl and did not understand what happened but she obediently told her parents what she saw and they were able to recognize the situation.

"The King of the Dwarfs wants to wed you," her father, Tomos, said.

"Me marry that little... little, um-" Lyneth stammered, not knowing the word she wanted, her forehead wrinkling in distaste.

"Oh dear. What shall we do?" her mother, Catrin said.

Tomos sat down wearily, "How much did he say the dowry was?"

"Tomos!" Catrin said.

Tomos shook his head and his eyes came back in focus,

"Don't worry my darlings, when that little man comes back I'll just tell him thanks but no thanks."

"I don't think it will be that easy. Kings are used to getting their own way," Catrin said, wringing her hands nervously.

"Aye, maybe you are right. I will ask the men their opinions on what to do."

As he said, Tomos went to the public house and told the men there what had happened.

Manus was the first to speak, "The King of Dwarfs is not one to trifle with. His magic is strong, there is no predicting what he will do if angered."

Kerwin said, "Aye, Dwarfs have tempers, and I'll wager the King of Dwarfs has a kingly one."

"What should I do?" Tomos asked.

The dozen or so patrons in the pub took a deep drink and stared at the floor.

"Galvin, what do you think I should do?" Tomos asked, a tone of desperation in his voice.

Galvin flushed slightly, uncomfortable with speaking in front of a crowd, then he spoke, "Dwarfs have a great respect for tradition. There are many stories of suitors being charged with three great tasks to perform before they are allowed to marry the princess. Pick three impossible tasks to prove his love. The king will have no choice but to give up his suit."

There was a moment of silence then a chorus of cheers, back slaps, and hurrahs.

"What shall the first task be?" Tomos asked, relief clear on his face.

There was another moment of silence, then the miller said, "Have him separate a bushel of wheat and bushel of oats that are all mixed together."

"In one night!" someone shouted.

"Aye! In one night," the miller added.

"What next?"

"Have him kill the giant Galifron!" the baker shouted, referring to a fierce and terrible giant that lives high up on the mountain.

"And the third task?"

"Make the shorty kiss her on the lips without a ladder." The men laughed. Tomos only glared.

"Make him cut down a tree with nothing but water," Kenhelm the carpenter said.

(indent) And so the list was decided. The night was getting late and the men began to drift out of the pub to wander back home.

"Oh thank you Galvin. Please, will you be at my house tomorrow when they come back? I don't know how to speak to a king," Tomos said as he and Galvin walked home.

"Certainly, I'd be happy to help," Galvin replied.

The next day at noon Arngrim appeared at the farmhouse along with a younger dwarf carrying a small but very heavy looking chest. He knocked on the door. Tomos answered.

Arngrim asked in an official voice devoid of emotion, "Are you the father or legal guardian of Lyneth, who is the most beautiful maiden of Bunwych?"

"Aye. Please come in," Tomos said wearily.

The two dwarfs entered the small farmhouse. They ignored Galvin who was seated at the kitchen table.

Arngrim coughed and with as much pomp as he could muster. "On behalf of his Royal Wideness, Gomrund the Magnificent, King of all the Dwarfs, I present the royal dowry." He stepped aside and motioned at the chest carrier, who, sweating and puffing, put the chest down on the table with a metallic clink.

Arngrim impatiently waved the servant aside, pulled a scroll out of his belt and held it up, letting it unfurl, touching the ground. "Here is the contract, your signature is required here, here, and... here."

"Excuse me, please, um-" Galvin interrupted Arngrim and scowled at him. "There is the matter of the tasks..."

"The what?"

"Only a small formality. It is customary in our culture that the father of the bride assign the betrothed three tasks which must be accomplished before the marriage can be granted. Here are the tasks, in written form." Before Arngrim could respond, Galvin stood up and thrust the paper into his hand.

Back in the dwarven throne room, Arngrim broke the news to the king.

"I, King of all the Dwarfs, am required to perform tasks like a pet dog! How dare they!" the king exclaimed, reaching for his ax out of habit. Cleverly, Arngrim had moved the ax to the other side of the room, out of the king's reach.

"It is part of their tradition, Your Wideness," Arngrim said.

Gomrund, being the king, was highly respectful of tradition. After all, it was what made the people follow and obey him. He sat back down, defeated.

"Yes, I suppose so. Now what is this first task I must perform?" the king said.

Arngrim lifted up his spectacles and held the paper up close to his eyes and read, "The groom must separate a bushel of wheat and a bushel of oats in one night. If one grain remains unsorted at sunrise, all rights of marriage to the bride must be forfeit."

"A bushel of wheat and a bushel of oats! That is impossible!" the king exclaimed.

"Difficult yes, impossible no. I have a plan, Your Wideness," Arngrim smiled mysteriously.

The Changeling

Liam sat in the tree cottage of Maeraedeth and eagerly opened the book to today's lesson.

Liam, you are now fourteen, nearly a man. The time has come to tell you what I have hidden from you. As you already know, you are not like the other elves, in fact, you are human. The faerie queen tricked your father, your real father, into making a pact. She gave him luck and wealth and in return she took you away when you were born and put in your place a goblin baby enchanted to look like you. You see, every seven years the queen must pay a tithe; a sacrifice to Cernunnos, Lord of the Forest. You were to be the sacrifice seven years ago. When I discovered this I arranged to hide you, and I offered myself to the queen in your place. Now it is time again and you must escape for she will not be foiled twice. Wait until midsummer's eve, the faeries will be distracted in their preparations for the ball. Read carefully, this is what you must do...

Two Weeks Before Midsummer's Eve

The First Impossible Task

And so the following day at dusk, Gomrund found himself alone in the barn of farmer Tomos looking up at a large pile of wheat and oats mixed together on the floor. Gomrund scrutinized the pile, scowled, and pulled out a piece of paper from his pocket which was prepared for him by his Minister of Magic. He read a simple incantation and performed a peculiar hand gesture. Then, he sat down on a hay bale and waited. Soon a scuttling, scratching sound could be heard, faint at first but soon growing in volume. Ants were entering the barn from every crack and seam in the walls and gathered before Gomrund, thousands strong. He stood up, cleared his throat, and addressed them, "I, King of the Dwarfs, command you to sort this grain, putting all the wheat here, and the oats there."

Immediately they obeyed. The king sat back down on the hay bale and watched. The undulating mass of maneuvering ants was hypnotic and soon he was fast asleep.

Outside, Arngrim, Tomos, Catrin, Galvin, and a few other men from the village waited nervously. The doors and windows were shut and all was quiet inside the barn. Lyneth was inside the house, asleep. She was certain her father would make the ugly little man go away, and didn't concern herself with the proceedings.

At last the cock crowed and dawn came.

The men entered the barn. The creaking noise of the large door opening caused the king to waken with a start and fall off his haystack.

The wheat was in one neat pile, but the oats were gone. The king stood there dumbfounded. Arngrim, Tomos, and Galvin stared at the lone pile. Arngrim noticed the horse had gotten out of its stall and guessed what had occurred. It just so happened that this horse, who was named Millie, adored oats but despised wheat.

"The task has been completed successfully. The wheat and the oats are separated. The wheat there, in the pile, and the oats in the belly of the horse," Arngrim said, ready for any objections. There were none, the village men just stood there sulking. King Gomrund stood there silently, blinking, still not quite awake.

"There, well, presently we shall return with the head of the giant Galifron," Arngrim continued. He touched his king's shoulder as a signal that they should leave.

Midsummer Festival

For the past three hundred or so years Bunwych has celebrated the midsummer festival. On Midsummer Eve it was a tradition that all the children of Bunwych under the age of sixteen are let out to play, frolic, romp, and do what they will. As long as they wear all white, they will not come to harm, for, on this the shortest night, all of the wicked creatures of the forest, caves, swamps, and barrows hide fearfully in their lairs. All adults must stay inside and have faith that their little ones will remain safe. In fact, no one could remember a time when a child came to any more harm than a bruise or scrape on this night. It is true that property such as a fence, wagon, or barn was occasionally damaged or a flower bed trampled. And sometimes a horse, chicken, or dog was disturbed, painted, loosed, shaved, plucked, or injured, but no serious damage was ever done.

At dawn the children would return, sweaty and exhausted, their eyes glassy with fatigue, their white clothing muddy and streaked with grass stains. Never would they reveal what they were up to and the adults were forbidden to ask. The actual activities were handed down from older siblings to younger siblings, and when the child turned sixteen they would mysteriously forget exactly what transpired during these nights, although they could still reminisce about these times with fondness.

On Midsummer Day the children would be allowed to sleep all day while the adults would gather in the village green in Inner Bunwych where there was feasting and dancing until dusk.

The four children of Wyn thought of little else weeks before the event. They would chatter amongst themselves about it excitedly but hush up when their mother came near enough to hear. Alec, at thirteen, was one of the leaders and planners of the event and took his responsibilities seriously.

It was a week before midsummer, midnight, and the children were all sound asleep. Through the warm, soft air, a bell would tinkle now and then from a cow or sheep off on the rolling pastures in the distance. In the windowsill, three shapes appeared, floating gently on the breeze like fluttering moths. They were pixies, scant five inches tall with white gossamer wings. They were looking at Julia, who was closest to the window.

"Is she the one?" one whispered.

"It is she," another answered.

"She is Bonny," the third added.

"Are you sure?" the first said.

"As sure as eggs is eggs," the second replied.

The first faerie then flew down and placed a small envelope in Julia's hand. She stirred and the pixies vanished in an instant. Julia woke and felt the envelope in her hand and held it up to the light of the half moon. It read, *Miss Julia*

She carefully opened it. Inside it read,

The honor of your company is requested at the Midsummer Ball.

Dawn Maidens, midnight

Perplexed but thrilled, she stuffed the invitation under her bed. This was faerie work, that much was obvious. The more she thought about it the more excited she grew. She took out the letter several times during the night to scrutinize it. There was one problem, what to wear? She certainly had no clothing suitable. Perhaps her mother had something that might fit, but she could not tell her about the ball. It must remain a secret, even to her brothers. Especially to them. She imagined the sweet faerie music, the lovely faerie maidens in their pretty gowns, the handsome faerie lads. Finally, an hour before dawn, she fell asleep.

The next day, while her mother was fetching water, Julia stole into her room and opened a large chest where her mother kept her finest dresses. She quickly was drawn to a sky blue frock peeking out tantalizingly from underneath a dozen other dresses. The material was sheer and so light as to be almost weightless. She held it up against her slim body. Perhaps a little big but some pins would rectify that. With a thrill of excitement she closed the chest and rushed up to her bedroom, carefully folding the dress and hiding it under her mattress.

The Wild Man

Alec had an argument with his mother. She wanted him to shell the beans but he was sick of beans and wanted to go to the river to fish. She tried to grab him for a thrashing but he was big now and too strong and too fast. In a rage, he ran off.

Alec went off into the forest, wandering for a while, his mind troubled. After a time he came to a secluded spot next to a craggy set of cliffs. There was a clear stream and he bent down to drink when he heard someone approaching. Instinctively, sensing danger, he crouched down low, hiding among the reeds.

A man approached the stream. He was unclothed except for a ragged fur loincloth, had hair and a beard that were very long and dark black, and a face that was deeply lined, although he didn't seem old. He carried a basket made out of the same reeds that Alec now hid in. The wild man stood on the bank of the stream and crouched down. After a few moments his hand darted into the stream and as quick as the wind, he grabbed a large fish and put it in the basket. The man calmly took the basket and turned and walked back the way he had come. As he passed near where Alec was hiding, he said, "Come speak to me and share my fish." He said this without pausing or looking at Alec and continued on his way, disappearing along a path which led toward the cliffs.

Intrigued, and not afraid, Alec stood up and followed. The path led to a small clearing in front of the cliff face where there was a small cave. Inside Alec could see a light from a fire. Alec hesitated. From inside the cave the wild man said, "Come, don't be afraid."

Alec stepped inside. The cave was about ten feet deep and obviously the home of the wild man. He was sitting down in front of a fire holding an iron pan. There was a loud sizzle as he placed the fish on the pan. Without looking at him the man said, "Sit."

"How did you catch the fish with your bare hands?" Alec asked.

"My will was stronger than the fish's," he replied.

"I don't understand," Alec said.

"You are young, there is much you don't understand," the wild man said without judgment as he flipped the fish with one deft motion of his hand.

"How old are you?" Alec asked.

The man laughed and took the pan away from the fire. He cut the fish with a knife and put half on a wooden board which he handed to Alec.

"Thank you," Alec said and began eating the fish with his hands just as the wild man was doing.

"Will you teach me how to catch fish like that?" he asked.

"That is why you are here," the man answered.

The man stood up and walked back towards the stream. He stopped and said to the boy, "Come."

He led the boy along a path leading back towards the forest. At last they came to a clearing near the face of the cliff. There was the stump of a large tree.

"Stand on this stump and do not move from it until I return," the wild man said.

Alec did as he was told and stood up on the stump. Hours passed and Alec grew very weary. The day grew long and Alec became angry that the wild man had left him there for so long. He got down from the stump and sat down on the ground, his back resting against the stump. "What does standing on a stump in the middle of a forest have to do with catching fish?" he asked himself.

Soon, without knowing it, Alec fell asleep. He was awakened by a great crashing sound coming from the same path they had taken. A big and fierce looking bear came running into the clearing. Alec screamed and ran for a nearby oak tree. He scrambled up the tree as the bear roared and attacked. As he was pulling himself up a branch the bear reached out with his great claw and raked his nails along Alec's leg. He climbed higher and was soon out of the bear's reach. The bear looked up at Alec and turned, going back the way he had come. Alec's leg wound was painful but not serious, still, he was bleeding a great deal.

A few minutes passed and the wild man emerged into the clearing from the same path as the bear. Alec climbed down.

"I commanded you to stay on the stump. Why were you up the tree?" he asked, not angry but disappointed.

"I was on the stump for many hours but then a great bear came and chased me up the tree," Alec said, not mentioning that he was sleeping on the ground before the bear attacked.

"Come," the wild man said.

He led the boy up the mountain to a clear spring which bubbled out of the rocks on the cliff side. There, he washed the boy's wound. As soon as the water touched his leg, the wound healed, although a golden colored scar remained.

They walked back to the wild man's camp. It was almost evening.

"I better go back. My mother will be worried," Alec said.

"No, if you wish to learn how to fish you must stay with me," the wild man said gently but firmly.

Alec wanted to stay but knew his mother would be worried and upset when he didn't return home before dark but somehow he sensed that staying was what he should do. He decided and sat back down.

That evening the wild man cooked some more fish and they ate some walnuts and green plants that grew along the stream. In front of the campfire the wild man told Alec many stories but they were different from the faerie stories his mother told him. These stories were about the beasts in the forest, the mountain, and the great storms and natural phenomena of the region.

The night was warm and they slept on a bed of moss outside of the cave by the fire.

When he awoke the next morning the wild man was gone. Alec got up, stoked the fire, and waited. Soon the wild man returned with another fish in his basket. They ate breakfast without speaking.

After breakfast the wild man led Alec along a path that led up the mountain. They came almost to the summit, to a precipice that jutted out a hundred feet above the wild man's cave.

"Go stand out on the rock and do not move from it until I return," the wild man said.

Alec walked out to the place the wild man pointed. He was afraid because a fall from this height would be fatal. He looked down and became dizzy, a feeling of panic seemed to issue from his heart and radiate out to his limbs, which grew weak.

He spied a rabbit down below. It was so far below him it looked tiny. Suddenly a memory rushed into his mind.

He was very small. His mother had left him alone in the house. She soon returned and grabbed him roughly and picked him up. She smelled strange. Suddenly they were in the air, flying. They were very high. He was so afraid, too afraid to even cry. Then there was a brilliant flash of light and he was violently rocked, then he was falling. Next, he remembered being on the ground in his mother's arms again. She was looking at him and crying. He began crying too.

He replayed the memory in his mind again. Now he could see the thing that grabbed him. It was not his mother. It was a monster too horrible for his young mind to contemplate.

He closed his eyes and calmed himself, then tilted his head back up and looked out over the valley. He could see the rolling green hills in the valley below and the fuzzy green carpet of the great forest far in the distance. He saw the river winding silently through the land like a great snake. His fear faded away and he felt a rush of well-being take its place.

There he stood for many hours. His legs grew weary but he ignored that. When he began to feel afraid he closed his eyes, breathed slowly and concentrated on the magnificent view.

Just then a huge red tailed hawk landed on a rock nearby, then disappeared over the ridge. Wanting to get a closer look at the magnificent creature, Alec crept closer. The hawk then flew off. There was a faint chirping sound. He walked closer and saw a nest with three hawk chicks, a few weeks old. Alec was fascinated and stood watching. He heard the hawk's cry and started to turn when the bird swooped down and scratched him on the forehead. Alec ducked and backed away from the nest. Just then he heard someone approaching and the wild man emerged from the path.

"Why did you not stay on the rock as I commanded?" he asked firmly but without anger.

"I was there for many hours but then I saw the hawk and was curious," Alec said, ashamed at failing the test.

The wild man seemed to accept this explanation and led Alec back down the mountain. Once again they stopped at the magical spring where he washed the wound on his forehead. And once again the wound was instantly healed, but a faint golden colored scar remained.

Back at the camp Alec asked, "Yesterday I stood on a stump, today I stood out on a cliff. What do these things have to do with fishing?"

The wild man replied, "Before you can learn to fish, you must learn how to stand."

That evening was much like the evening before except instead of a fish, the wild man cooked a rabbit he had caught in a snare. He taught Alec the proper way to tend a fire, how to make fire with a stick and a bow, and how to make a campfire last all night without having to be tended to.

The next morning the wild man led Alec down to the stream where he had been fishing the day before.

He said, "Stand here in this stream and watch the fish until I return. Do not try to catch one or put your hands in the water."

Alec did as he was told and stood in the cool stream, unmoving. Occasionally a large fish would swim by. The hours passed and although his legs remained strong, his mind grew weary. A large fish appeared just below him in his reach. Without thinking he bent down and grabbed at the fish but it was slippery and fell immediately through his hands. The water was cold and numbed his hands slightly. He looked at them and saw that they had turned a golden color, like the scars on his legs and forehead.

The wild man soon returned. He looked at Alec's hands and said, "I commanded you to stand in the stream and not reach into the water. Why have you disobeyed?"

Alec was ashamed. He looked down and said, "I am sorry. I thought I could catch the fish. It was so close."

"You have failed each task I have given you, but you have made a good start and I am pleased. You must leave me now and go back to the world, but if you ever have need of me, just stand on the edge of the forest and call for me three times and I will come and help you."

Alec was surprised but pleased that the man said he had made a good start, and followed the trail back home, his mind clear and content.

When his mother saw him, much to his surprise, she didn't yell or even ask him where he had been or why his hands were golden. All she did was hug him tightly, not saying a word.

Four Days Before Midsummer's Eve

The Goblin Servant

In Inner Bunwych, in the heart of the town center, lived an old man named Galvin. He was the town apothecary once but was now retired. He lived in a fine house made of stone and brick with two stories but was too poor to hire servants.

Galvin was never married and had no children. Sitting by the fire on winter nights alone he thought often about his own death and the meaning of his life. True, he helped nurse many villagers back to health with the medicines and herbs he sold, but he wanted to leave something behind that was more permanent, more substantial. After much reflection, an idea came to him and he made a decision. He would bestow his house and books to the village and found the first library in the history of Bunwych. The thought of leaving his beloved house and even more beloved books to be used by generations of future Bunwychians gave him great peace and solace. He wouldn't tell anyone just yet, there was no hurry.

One day he was carrying wood in from the shed and thought to himself, I wish I had someone here to help me do these things.

He retired to bed and slept soundly. The next morning he awoke to find the house inexplicably clean. The ashes had been swept out of the fireplace. The dishes had been washed and put away. The towel was cleaned and dried. The books in his library were all put away. The floors were free of dirt.

He was mystified but calm because after all, strange things often happened in Bunwych. He sat down at the kitchen table sipping some milk when the back door opened.

In came a little man, three feet tall, with a long pointed

nose and sharp chin, wearing humble gray clothing. He was a type of faerie called a goblin.

"Greetings, Master. I have brought you some currant buns for your breakfast," he said casually.

"Who are you?" Galvin asked, astonished.

The little man bowed and said, "My name is Dozank Mithagoar, I am the new servant you requested."

"Requested? But I am poor. I have nothing to pay your salary."

"That matters not. All I require is a crust of stale bread in the evening. I can sleep in the attic and eat the mice I find."

Galvin knew in the back of his mind that faeries always demand payment, but he was so eager to have a servant that he pushed this thought aside.

Galvin spent that day propped up on his favorite chair while Dozank rearranged the furniture, brought in water from the well, neatly stacked the firewood, planted a new row of roses, and washed all the linens. In the evening Galvin dismissed his servant and went to bed while Dozank disappeared up the creaky stairs to the attic and never made a sound all night. Galvin smiled and felt a warmth of contentment spread over him as he dozed off.

The next morning came filled with birdsong. Galvin dressed and went to the kitchen expecting his faerie servant to be there awaiting him. Instead, there were two faeries.

"This is my brother Zabark Shadowmantle." The new faerie, who looked exactly like the original one, bowed courteously. "He will be helping me with my duties. I hope that is satisfactory?"

Galvin, still not quite awake, blinked, and said, "Well, yes, I suppose so."

That day the two faeries dug a new well, washed the curtains, swept the floors, white washed the fence, and weeded the garden. Whilst outside they always kept invisible, much to Galvin's relief, for he would have been quite embarrassed if the neighbors knew he had goblin servants doing his work for him.

It was a giant, at least thirty feet high, with tusks like a boar, and wore a rough tunic of ragged and filthy furs.

Terrell's Expedition

Terrell and his men were now in mountainous territory. Terrell heard a sound and stopped so quickly that the man behind him bumped into him. He held his hand up, listening. Again he heard the sound, it was the distinct "baaa" of a goat. They were nearly out of provisions and fresh meat would be a godsend. They followed the sound into a cleft in the mountain with great boulders surrounding them on three sides. There at the back was the goat, just standing there. Terrell stopped, and as his men rushed by him, he noticed the rope. The goat was tied to a stump. He was about to shout a warning when the ground gave way and all five men plunged into a pit. They cried out in pain and anger.

Terrell felt the ground tremble slightly. "Quiet! Be quiet!" He shouted to the men and there was an eerie stillness. Again the tremble, slightly stronger this time, accompanied by a great crashing of underbrush, as if a dozen men were approaching. He quickly dove for cover, behind some brush just as the monster appeared through the trees. It was a giant, at least thirty feet high, with tusks like a boar, and wore a rough tunic of ragged and filthy furs. Quickly it came to the pit and looked down.

"Wot! Men?! It's me lucky day!" it said in a voice deep and rumbling like distant thunder.

Terrell watched with horror as the giant plucked the men one at a time out of the pit, tied them together by their feet then slung them around his shoulder. He felt like fleeing and not looking back but instead Terrell gathered his courage and followed the giant as it quickly wound its way up the mountain with its huge strides. The giant passed out of sight and Terrell broke into a run, catching a glimpse of the monster as it disappeared into a cave. He hesitated. What fool would dash into a dark cave? Surely the men were already dead. Even outside the cave he could smell the stench from inside, it was the smell of death. He thought of his uncle, doubtless he would go in. If he fled, could he face his father and tell him the truth?

The knight drew his sword and entered the cave. He paused for a few moments at the entrance, allowing his eyes to adjust to the darkness. Blinking, he could make out the dim light of a fire inside, and hear the moans of his men echoing up the tunnel. Keeping his back to the wall, Terrell cautiously descended deeper into the cave.

He could see the back of the giant, who was bending down at the fire. Terrified but resolved, Terrell charged, raising his sword to plunge into the giant's back. In the darkness, he kicked a stone and stumbled. The giant heard, turned, and swung an arm the size of a large tree trunk into Terrell's chest. He blacked out.

The Second Impossible Task

King Gomrund restlessly paced his throne room while Arngrim, his adviser, did his best to keep up.

"How soon can my army kill this giant?" the king asked impatiently.

"Forgive me sire, but the contract states that you and you alone must defeat the giant," Arngrim replied.

"What! I am no warrior! How am I to kill a giant?"

"Fear not my liege, I have a plan. We must go to the treasure room."

King Gomrund and Arngrim walked down the long hallway which wound down deep under the earth, their footsteps echoing against the cold damp stone. They came to a door and the king held up the enormous ring of keys he was carrying and picked one out. He opened the lock and the two proceeded down another hallway. They came to twelve more locked doors and the lock was always opened by a different key. At last they came to the final and largest door, a massive round door made of thick oak and reinforced with iron straps. The king held up the keys to the light of the lantern Arngrim was carrying and took out the largest, then put the key in the lock and with a metallic clank, the door unlocked. The door squealed as he opened it, as if in pain. They beheld a large natural cavern filled with chests of all manner of sizes, styles, and composition. There were also other various items strewn about; bejeweled swords, plates, furs, shields, casks, barrels, even a large golden harp.

Arngrim held up the lantern and said, "Now the item should be here in this chest."

He put the lantern down and opened the chest. Inside was an item about the size of a book, kept inside a bag made of crimson velvet.

"Ah, yes. This, my lord, is the mirror of petrifaction," Arngrim said, holding the artifact with great care and respect.

"What is that?" the king scowled, for he hated long words.

"A magical mirror my lord, which turns whoever gazes into it into stone. It was found by your great grandfather Bodram Ironchain when he defeated the dragon Nagendra."

"Ah, I see your plan. All I need to do is show the mirror to the giant and he will be destroyed."

"Yes, but please, my lord, be careful not to look into the mirror yourself, or you yourself will be turned to stone," Arngrim said.

Terrell Is Captured

Terrell slowly opened his eyes, careful not to move or make a sound. He and two of his men were on a narrow ledge overlooking a vast chasm, hundreds of feet deep and twelve feet wide, too far to jump. The other men were still. He could see one of their faces, the eyes were open but blank. He was dead. Slowly, he turned so he could see the other man. His back was bent at a sickening, unnatural angle. The smooth walls were slick with water and very slippery, impossible to climb. There was a fire just on the other side of the chasm. It was large in area but what remained of the fire were only a few glowing coals. The corpses of three men were next to the fire, stacked neatly.

The giant returned carrying an armful of green leaves. He then proceeded to grab one of the corpses and tear off its clothing, then took a nearby pole and impaled the man through it from mouth to arse. Thereupon he placed the pole between some rocks such that the body was balanced just above the fire at a 45 degree angle. He repeated this with the two remaining corpses, then placed the bundle of leaves atop the glowing coals. Very soon, thick gray smoke billowed out, rising up into the air through the three men and up into the air.

Terrell was sickened by this display of culinary horror and had to fight back a wave of nausea.

The giant then proceeded to rub each of the corpses with what looked like a strip of fat. Then, he put his hand into a sack and sprinkled each body with some kind of pepper.

Terrell had a notion, "I congratulate you on your careful preparation of the meat."

The giant seemed surprised that one of his prisoners spoke to him. He stared for a moment then returned to his work.

He tried again. "Who taught you how to cook?"

The giant stopped again and stared. He answered in a coarse, deep voice. "It were me muvver wot taught me."

"Excellent. I see you are smoking the meat."

"Yar, it gives the flesh a nice flavor and it will stay for weeks. Yer 'ave ter use wet leaves, right, else it will burn and not smoke."

"Very impressive. I also am a cook. I am the king's royal chef as a matter of fact."

"Wot? You was the cook for the king of all the land?"

"Yes, I have served him many meals."

The giant took a step to the edge of the chasm and sat down, letting his legs dangle over the cliff.

"Wot dishes does 'e like best?"

"Oh, his tastes are varied. Sometimes mutton, sometimes pheasant pie, sometimes roast pig, but his favorite is royal soup."

"royal soup? Wot's dat?"

"Oh, that is a delicious soup made from some very special herbs and pig stock, but any type of meat will do."

The giant smacked his lips, "Dat sounds delicious! Tell me the recipe!"

"Oh, I don't know. The king would be very cross if I divulged his secret favorite recipe."

"Tell me or I'll rip yor left arm off!"

"Very well. If you insist. First, get that cauldron over there and fill it with water.

Eagerly, the giant got up, picked up the cauldron and loped up the tunnel to fetch water from outside.

As soon as the giant was out of sight, Terrell burst into feverish activity. He began tearing long strips of fabric from the pants of his comrades, and tied them together. He had twenty feet of rope ready when he heard the giant returning and stuffed the rope behind one of the men and resumed the position he was in when the giant left.

"Got the water. Right, wot next?"

"Now place the pot over some flame and let the water heat up."

Eagerly Galifron obeyed, arranging some rocks to place the pot on and putting more firewood in the middle of the rocks. Then he took a glowing brand from the fire and placed it in the new fire and soon the flames were licking up over the pot.

"Now wot?"

"Put the meat in the pot."

"Right!" The giant then took one of the skewered men and slid him into the pot.

Terrell hoped the giant didn't notice his grimace at gruesome treatment of his dead comrade.

"What else?"

"Next throw in some onions."

The giant disappeared behind a rock and came out with a bag. He emptied the bag of onions into the pot.

"Ah, now this is the most important part, put in a few handfuls of Aconitum napellus roots."

"Agony wot?"

"Don't tell me you don't know about Aconitum napellus?"

"Wot? Ya I 'erd of it, course I 'erd of it. I just don't 'ave any."

"That is not a problem. I saw some growing just outside the cave."

"Oh, right, uh, wot's it look like? I forgot."

"The one with the purple flowers, pull it up and take the

roots. Get a good couple of handfuls."

"Right, right." Galifron was excited, and fairly skipped away to the cave entrance.

When the giant returned he held up two handfuls of roots for the human's approval.

Terrell said, "Good. Now just toss them in the pot."

The giant did so, then said, "Now wot?"

"In about an hour it should be ready," Terrell replied.

"Right." The giant then sat down in front of the pot and stared at it patiently.

Just at that moment, King Gomrund, Arngrim and two other dwarfs from court were at the entrance to the cave of Galifron.

The king was very frightened but was careful to not let his subjects see it. He left the group and marched boldly into the cave, holding the velvet bag with the mirror of petrifaction in both hands. He stepped inside. The cave was damp and he immediately noticed the smell of smoke mingling with the horrible stench of death. He ducked behind a rock to catch his breath and let his eyes become accustomed to the darkness. Gathering his courage, he continued on. He could hear voices coming from deeper in the cave. Were there two giants? He wondered with dread. No way to turn back and save his honor. He continued on.

He heard heavy footsteps approaching very quickly.

The king's blood turned to ice and his feet became very heavy. He turned to run but there was no place to hide. Then, he remembered the magic mirror and the plan. He opened the bag, thrust his hand in and pulled out the mirror. It was very shiny. He was holding the mirror the wrong way! The reflective surface was pointed at him! Luckily he did not look directly into it. The giant was closer, he could just see it now, coming out of the gloom.

With shaky, panicky hands he turned the mirror around, but it slipped and flew out of his hands. The mirror landed with a crash and shattered into a hundred pieces.

The king threw himself down on his knees and cried, "Please, mighty giant, spare me! I meant no harm!"

Terrell emerged from the gloom of the smokey cavern, his eyes blinking in the rays of sunshine gleaming from the cave entrance ahead. "Fear not little man. The giant is slain," he said.

Gomrund looked up at the tall human, "You are not the giant?" he asked, the words both a statement and a question.

"No. The giant you seek lies in there, dead as a stone," Terrell said.

With that, the king exclaimed a strange yelp of delight, sprang to his feet, and ran deeper into the cave.

"Madman," Terrell said to himself as he watched the dwarf disappear down the tunnel, then continued on exiting the cavern.

This is what had happened. The hour of cooking time had elapsed, and the giant eagerly tasted his soup. "Delicious!" he exclaimed, then greedily ate more and more. Very soon the soup was all eaten up and the giant sat down, his hunger satisfied. He then grasped at his belly and said, "I think I ate too much!"

Those were his final words. The deadly monkshood had done its job and poisoned the giant.

When he saw the giant was dead, Terrell instantly jumped up and grabbed his rope. His only chance was to throw the end of the rope attached to the boot in such a way as to wedge it between two large rocks. It took many tries, but this he did. Then he held the rope taught, and let himself swing to the other ledge. He was dreadfully bruised when he hit the wall, but managed to hold on to the rope. All was needed then was to climb up the rope to safety.

He paused for a moment at the giant's treasure hoard. It was hardly a king's ransom. There was no gold, only old worthless junk and baubles of little value. But there were some silver and copper coins which Terrell stuffed into his pockets. He was about to leave when a glint caught his eye. Pulling away an old moldy tapestry revealed a fine longsword, which he pulled out of the pile. The sword shined brightly in the dim light of the dying fire. It looked silver but was very light and no tarnish marred its surface. He tested its strength by laying the point against the ground and putting his weight on it. He could bend it only slightly and it sprang back immediately. It was the finest sword he had ever seen. He found a scabbard and put it on his belt.

Terrell emerged out of the cave blinking, blinded from the light. In a few moments his vision returned and he spied the river down below, winding snakelike between the forest on the far edge of the river and the pale green fields of Bunwych; criss crossed with deeper green bands of hedgerows. The yellow limestone cottages of the village proper could be seen far in the distance, as well as a large structure which must be the castle.

He started down the mountain, not seeing the frightened dwarfs who were hiding in the bushes.

King Gomrund saw the giant ahead, slumped against the wall. In a moment of panic he was frightened and turned to flee, but then realized that the giant was indeed dead. The plan was to take the giant's head but he could see now it would be far too heavy to carry. He decided the giant's smallest finger would have to do. He swung the ax with all his might and barely nicked the bone. The body shifted slightly and the king dropped the ace and ran in panic for the exit but after a few strides he could hear nothing behind him and regained his confidence. Seven more blows were needed to sever the finger.

King Gomrund emerged from the cave, triumphantly holding up the little finger of the dead giant. His entourage came out of their hiding place and gave three cheers to their mighty king.

He explained that the mirror had failed and the giant swatted it out of his hands, destroying it. Personal combat followed, and more than once the giant had almost got the better of the dwarf, but with great skill and courage, he managed to defeat the giant. The man who walked out of the cave, Gomrund explained, was some poor human the king rescued from the giant's prison. This is how Gomrund acquired his newest moniker "The Giant Slayer."

The Swan Faerie

Morris was told by Wyn to clean out the chicken coop. This he truly meant to do but was distracted by a magnificent stick lying in the path. It was straight and tapered, perfect for sword play. He picked it up and ran into the woods to practice foyning on the pass and coup de main, soon finding himself far from the house by a large marsh.

Just then he heard a great commotion from up ahead. He ran and saw a fox attacking a white swan who had got itself stuck in a briar. The swan was honking and struggling with its wings but was getting even more tangled the more it struggled. The fox was lunging at it and at any moment would kill the helpless swan.

Morris sprang into action, running to the fox, yelling his loudest and brandishing the stick at it. The fox was startled by the boy and ran off into the woods. The swan became calm and stopped struggling. Morris crawled into the briar bush and carefully pulled the branches apart, then pulled out the lovely white bird which allowed itself to be rescued.

The swan took a few steps, shook itself, turned to face the boy and transformed into a beautiful maiden. She wore a downy white gown which clung closely to her body and hung down to her knees. Her feet were bare.

"Thank you," she said, bowing to the boy.

"Who are you? Are you a swan or a woman?" Morris asked.

"I am the Swan Faerie. I live in the marsh," she said, her voice full of kindness and love.

She bent down and touched him on the shoulder affectionately. "For your bravery I shall reward you. Come with me," she said.

She took Morris by the hand and led him down to the edge

of the marsh.

"Wait here," she said and took a step into the water. She transformed back into a swan at once.

She swam towards the middle of the marsh and dove under the water. After a few seconds she emerged again, holding something in her beak. She swam back to the shore and changed back into a woman, holding a red felt cap in her hand.

"This is a cap of invisibility. When you put it on, none can see you. You may someday find it useful." She handed it to Morris.

"Thank you," Morris said.

"If you ever need my help, come to my lake and call for me and I will come." With that, she bent down and kissed the boy on the cheek, then transformed back into a swan. She rose up into the sky, did a few circles high above, then disappeared over the horizon.

Morris looked down at the simple felt hat and frowned, skeptical that it would work. He put on the cap. I don't feel different, he thought to himself. He looked at his hands then down at his body and saw only the bare ground. He was invisible! But what good was being invisible when there was no one else around? A clever notion popped into his head. He would find his sister and play a trick on her.

Nessa was by the cottage playing with the rabbits. She had Sir Cabbage on her lap and was stroking it lovingly.

Still wearing the cap of invisibility, Morris crept up behind her and said in a funny little voice, "Thank you for petting me. You are very kind."

Nessa was so surprised she almost dropped the bunny. "I never knew you could talk, Sir Cabbage!"

"I was human once. A wicked faerie cast a spell on me and turned me into a rabbit," Morris said.

"I must help you break the spell so you can become a handsome prince again!" Nessa said. She then kissed the rabbit.

Morris wanted desperately to laugh but managed to suppress it with great difficulty.

"To break the spell you must bathe me in an enchanted spring in the forest," he said.

"Show me where!" Nessa said, standing up and facing the forest eagerly.

"That way!" Morris said.

Morris led her through the forest, staying just behind her and encouraging her all the way.

At last they came to the spring Morris had selected. It was a rocky hill with clear water bubbling down from the rocks.

"This is it! Now bathe me in the water and the spell will be broken!" Morris said.

Nessa knelt down and shoved the rabbit under the cool trickling water. The instant she did this the startled Sir Cabbage gave a great kick and broke free from her grip, and then, as fast as the wind on a wild tom cat, darted off into the brush.

"Sir Cabbage!" Nessa cried out and chased after it.

Morris, unable to contain his laughter, was doubled over and lay there helpless for a time.

After a few moments, Morris regained his composure and stood up. Nessa was gone without a trace.

He quickly ran off in the direction he thought she went. Seeing what looked like her small footprints in the mud, he stopped and called out, "Nessa!"

Then, remembering that he still had on the cap of invisibility, he tore it off so she could see it was her brother and called her again, "Nessa!"

There was no answer. This was a dark part of the forest their mother had forbid them to enter. Morris was beginning to panic, but then he remembered what the swan faerie said and ran for the lake as fast as he could.

His heart pounding, and his lungs starved, he reached the edge of the marsh but was too exhausted to call out. When he regained his breath, but still not able to stand, he called out, "Swan Faerie! Swan Faerie! I need your help!"

A few moments passed, then again, "Please Swan Faerie, help me!"

Then at last, from up in the sky swooped down a beautiful swan. She landed gracefully on the water then transformed into her human form and waded to shore.

"What's wrong, dear one?" She bent down and touched Morris' hands.

"My sister has vanished and it is my fault. Please help me find her," Morris said, still gulping for breath.

They came to a dark and swampy part of the forest and Morris could see an ancient looking hut made with gnarled branches, mossy rocks, and dried mud. The roof was thatch, but so ancient that small, evil looking scrubs grew from it.

The Witch

The swan faerie instantly became a swan again and took off into the air. Morris sat there and watched her circle high up above the forest. After a few minutes she returned, landing in front of Morris and becoming human again. She had a grave look on her face.

"She has been snatched by the witch that lives in the deepest part of the forest. You must hurry, for she means your sister no good. Follow me, I will show you where to go, but be careful. She is very dangerous."

She became a swan again and took off quickly into the sky.

Morris followed, trying to keep sight of her through the branches high above. The swan circled up in the sky, allowing Morris to keep up.

They came to a dark and swampy part of the forest and Morris could see an ancient looking hut made with gnarled branches, mossy rocks, and dried mud. The roof was thatch, but so ancient that small, evil looking scrubs grew from it.

The swan swooped down and landed by the boy.

"I am sorry I cannot help you for her magic here is more powerful than mine. Have you the cap I gave you?"

Morris nodded and pulled the hat out of his pocket.

"Good, put it on and be brave and be clever," she said, then quickly took off for the open sky.

Morris put the cap on and crept closer to the hut. He saw an open window and cautiously peered inside.

With relief he spied his sister inside, sitting on a little stool, alive and well. Before her was the witch. She was ancient, stooped, and gnarled. Her hair was black and gray and she wore no hat. Her clothing was a long, black gown, torn in many places.

Nessa was looking up at her. She didn't seem very afraid but was grave and suspicious.

The witch handed her a bowl and said, "Eat up this milk and don't be afraid." Her voice seemed kind, but Morris could sense the evil in her.

"Thank you," Nessa said, and took the bowl. Morris wanted to shout to her to not eat what the witch was giving her, but wisely held his tongue.

"Tomorrow, after you have rested, I will take you home to your mother," the witch said.

"Thank you," Nessa said.

"Now, wait here and don't be afraid my dear, I will be back in a moment. I just need to bring in some firewood," the witch said, and turned to walk out the door but before she left she stopped at a large cobweb in the corner of the room. She held out a gnarled hand to a huge black spider, touched it gently and whispered something to it. Then, she left and walked around to the other side of the hut.

Seeing his opportunity, Morris ran to the door and entered the hut, being as quiet as he could. He passed by the crow sized spider warily, which twitched a bit but did not move to stop him. Then, he came to Nessa, who had no idea he was there and whispered to her.

"Nessa, do not be afraid, it is your brother Morris."

"Morris! But why can't I see you?" she said, altogether too loudly.

"Quiet! Or the witch will hear. Now listen-" Just then he heard the witch coming back.

He backed into a corner and was still.

The hag came back in carrying a big armful of firewood.

She put most of them into the fire which quickly grew fierce and hot.

"There, now, we will have a nice hot supper this evening." She turned to look at Nessa. She seemed to sense something. Her eyes narrowed and she took a step closer. She turned her head in the direction Morris was hiding and sniffed the air. Morris' blood curdled with fright, but he remained still. She took another step closer, her cloudy eyes looking right through Morris, who was now certain that she could see him.

Just then Nessa began to cry and said, "I want to go home."

The witch turned around, the child's crying abruptly changed her manner, all pretense of kindness now vanished.

"Be quiet!" she said fiercely.

At the harsh words, Nessa became defiant, glaring crossly at the witch.

She shouted, "I want to go home now!"

"Stop it! I detest the sound of human young crying!" she shrieked, holding her ears.

Of course, this did not stop her, so the witch ran over to a cupboard and took out a rag. This she used to gag Nessa with.

"That's better."

Beside the fireplace was an enormous oven with a metal door. The witch picked up a straw brush and opened the door. She leaned inside and started to brush it out.

Seeing his chance, Morris didn't hesitate. He ran up and pushed her right into the oven, then closed and latched the door.

A hideous shriek came from inside the oven. Morris quickly grabbed his sister's hand and pulled her up. They ran to the door, but the spider had jumped down and was blocking the way. He grabbed a broom that was within reach and swatted the spider, knocking it across the room. They ran past it, out the door, and did not look back.

When they were far away from the hut Morris took off the cap and embraced his sister. Fearing the wrath from his mother, he made her promise to not breathe a word of this to anyone. Being grateful for her rescue, and also knowing that she had broken a promise to never enter the dark forest alone, she gladly agreed to keep the matter a secret.

The Dwarf King Returns a Hero

Gomrund strutted down the great hall like a rooster who had just chased off a killer hawk. Word of the king's glory had preceded him and a crowd of dwarfs lined the sides of the hall to pay homage. At first, like true dwarfs, they were quiet and respectful. Then, a bold young dwarf lad called out, "Hail Gomrund the giant slayer!"

The crowd cheered in response and the atmosphere turned raucous and people rushed toward the king, patting his back, and renewing the cheers. For his part, the king turned red and beamed with pride.

Gomrund entered the private antechamber to the throne room, followed by Arngrim. He sat down on the throne, this one cushioned and more comfortable than the one in the true throne room. He put his feet up on the foot rest and sighed contentedly while Arngrim waited patiently.

Finally, he said, "Now, Arngrim, what is the last task of the contract?"

Arngrim started, "You-" His voice was hoarse and he cleared his throat and started again, "You are to take down the tallest tree in Bunwych with nothing but water."

Gomrund slowly turned to his adviser and watched him for a moment. "And what is your plan to achieve this impossible sounding task?"

"Simple, my lord. You shall use an ice ax to take down the tree."

"And where will we find ice in the peak of summertime?"

"That part of the plan will be carried out by an ice drake."

"An ice drake! Where shall we find one of those?"

"There is one in the Gelid Chasm, deep below our feet,

but do not concern yourself with those details. That part of the task can be accomplished by your loyal subjects."

The king frowned as he thought about this, then stood up and said, "No Arngrim, I shall personally complete this task myself. I have grown fond of danger and glory. I feel like a two hundred year old again!" Curiously, the king suffered what could be called selective amnesia. He had forgotten the terrible moment of sheer panic when he dropped the magical mirror and heard the giant approaching, remembering only the feeling of triumph when he hacked of the giant's thumb and the adulation of the court when he returned.

Arngrim had misgivings but didn't bother to try to change his lord's mind. He knew his stubbornness too well.

Julia

Terrell Arrives

Lord Terrell, knowing that his destination was in sight, cheerfully followed the river bank. The way was clear of nettles and thorns, as if the gods of the forest welcomed him now.

After following the river for most of the day, Terrell reached the outermost edge of Bunwych. He spied a cottage through the trees and eagerly made for it. He was famished. It so happened that it was the cottage of Wyn and her four children.

Just outside the cottage was a clothesline on which was hung the family rug. Julia was in the act of beating it with a wicker switch. It was a chore she enjoyed because she always imagined the area she was hitting was the backside of her brother's trousers. With each swing, a great puff of dust emanated from both sides of the rug. Her hair was tied back and a rag was wrapped around her head. Her face was streaked with dirt from the rug.

Terrell approached but she was facing the other way. He called out to her but she couldn't hear him over her beating. Circling around to the side, he smiled and said greetings. She screamed and raised the beater as if to attack, then saw the young man smiling.

"I am terribly sorry for giving you a fright," Terrell said and bowed.

Notwithstanding the ragged appearance of his clothing, Julia could tell by his manner and speech and fine sword that he was a gentleman, and a handsome one at that. She dropped the beater and looked down shyly, self consciously brushing dust from her frock.

"I have been traveling for days. May I buy a bit of spare food from your larder?" he asked.

"Wait here," she said in a tiny voice and rushed inside.

Wyn was inside, kneading dough for bread. Nessa was also there, sitting on her little chair and drawing with chalk on a piece of slate.

"Mother! There is a stranger outside who wants to buy some food," Julia whispered urgently.

"So invite him in," Wyn answered.

Julia was now busy washing her face in the wash tub and ignored her command.

"Never mind, I'll do it," Wyn said.

Julia saw her mother leaving then rushed up the ladder to her bedroom.

Wyn said to the stranger, "Please, won't you come in?"

Terrell beheld a beautiful woman with nut-brown hair, of middling height, with a friendly but mysterious smile, and common peasant clothes although she moved with the grace of a princess.

He entered and she motioned to a seat, "Please sit down."

Nessa looked up and grinned widely at the stranger who grinned back.

Wyn took down a wooden bowl and spooned into it the leftover oatmeal from the morning and set it in front of him. He immediately began eating ravenously. She studied him as he ate.

"Oh my, you are hungry," Wyn said.

"This is the village called Bunwych, is it not?"

"Oh yes, well, Outer Bunwych; the town proper is just down the road over the bridge."

"I have heard Bunwych has a fine castle, is that true?"

Wyn laughed. "The castle is but a ruin. No one has lived there for many years."

Nessa walked up beside him and looking up, asked, "Are

you a knight?"

Wyn laughed again, "Nessa," she scolded.

"Forgive me, my name is Terrell and yes I am indeed one of the king's knights."

Wyn's eyes narrowed slightly. She detected a lie, although she would have never guessed that he was under exaggerating his status as a prince. "I am Wyn and this is Nessa," she replied.

Julia had just emerged from her room, her face washed, hair brushed, and wearing her best dress. The transformation took only a few minutes which impressed her mother greatly.

"And this is my daughter Julia," she added.

Julia curtsied and her face reddened.

"Please have some more," Wyn said, noticing that he was almost finished with the oatmeal. She took down a loaf of bread, a dish with some butter, and a jug of milk.

"I am grateful," he said, and began eating the bread.

"What brings you to Bunwych, Sir Terrell?" Wyn probed.

"A mission from the king," he said between mouthfuls of bread.

Julia took the empty bowl from the table and took it to the sink where she pretended to wash it.

"Are you going to live here with us?" Nessa asked.

He stopped eating for a moment in surprise, and looked down at her in a kindly way. "Well, if by that you mean will I be living in Bunwych, then yes, as least for a time."

He finished the bread and raised the jug of milk, drinking it without pause until it was drained.

Wyn held up a tiny bottle of ointment. "This will help take away the nettles rash on your hands." Terrell smiled and nodded and Wyn rubbed some gently onto his hand. Julia quietly fumed.

"My thanks. The itching is gone already," he said and smiled at Wyn.

"Do you have a spare lamp and some oil I may buy?" Terrell asked.

"Will you be going to the castle this evening?" Wyn asked as she fetched the things.

"Yes, why?"

"The castle is haunted," Julia answered, turning to look at the young knight with grave concern.

Terrell laughed. "I have come too far to be turned back by ghosts, my lady," he said.

"I am grateful for your kind hospitality," he said and bowed to Wyn. Then he placed a few copper coins on the table, patted Nessa on the head and left.

Wyn picked up a coin and studied it. It was ancient, had the image of a king many years dead and buried and was long since out of circulation.

This young knight is very mysterious, she thought to herself as she watched him through the window.

When he was out of sight she sighed and said to Julia, still looking out the window, "You can go take off the dress now and get back to your chores."

The Castle

Terrell followed the path which led to a road alongside the river. He could see the distant castle on the other side of the river. Soon he reached the bridge leading into Bunwych. The town was charming, although some of the buildings were in poor repair. Most of the houses were timber framed with stucco walls and thatched roofs. A few of the larger houses were made of tan colored stone bricks and slate roofs, but these looked older and were more dilapidated, often with missing tiles on the roof. He passed several townspeople who stopped and stared at him as he smiled and walked by. Passing through the center of town heading north, the town soon gave way to fields, then an orchard, which was poorly tended and allowed to spread wild to the very walls of the castle.

The outer castle walls were almost completely destroyed. Some sections were missing entirely. Villagers no doubt borrowed these stones to build houses and walls in other parts of the town. Passing through, he saw that the inner walls fared better, although there were large sections breached and crumbling. Still, it was repairable, he noted. As he passed through the two towers which once made up the gatehouse, several wild dogs fled through numerous holes in the wall. Here, in the inner courtyard, weeds grew in bunches through the crumbling paving stones. He noted deer droppings there as well.

Within the inner walls was the keep. This large, square building was in better condition but still sorely neglected. Vines had invaded the outer walls, creeping all the way to the roof in places. Part of the roof was caved in, along with a section of the south wall which would have been the main entrance to the castle.

He continued to walk around the keep, looking for a way inside. At the east wall was a set of eight enormous arched doorways, the doors of which were completely missing. It was not a good feature defensively but the view must have been impressive. The castle was no doubt constructed during a more peaceful time than now, he mused. Facing away from the keep toward the river he could see the remnants of a long neglected lawn and garden and wished he could have seen the view in its heyday.

As he stepped into the building a large vulture who had made its nest inside was startled and flew off, its massive wings beating the air with mighty whooshes. He was in what would have been the grand ballroom. The lofty, vaulted ceilings were largely intact, but much of the plaster had fallen off the walls into mounds of white snow-like powder. Mean scraps of furniture were strewn about along with animal droppings, nesting material, and bones. Weeds, moss, and even small trees were growing inside. The centerpiece of the room was a cascading stairway with its finely carved, marble balustrade flaring out into the room. He bent down and examined a small remaining scrap of carpet. It was red. He mounted the stairway which split into north and south curving sections.

On the second floor was a hallway leading to some rooms that no longer had floors. The third floor, which was doubtless the living quarters, was in better condition. There he found what must have been the king's bedroom with intact door, floor, and walls. Incredibly, the bed was still there, no doubt being too massive to steal easily.

It was past dark now and Terrell was exhausted. He lay down on the bed, not even bothering to undress and was instantly asleep.

Back in her bed, Julia could not sleep. She tossed and fretted as thoughts flooded her mind. Why did he have to come when she was looking so horrid? Did he call her my lady or was he talking to her mother? Is her mother interested in the handsome knight? What if he is married? Surely he will be destroyed by the ghosts of the castle. The idea that monsters may at this very moment be tearing him apart drove her mad. Finally, as the night grew long she fell asleep and dreamed.

By this time everyone in the village had learned of the stranger and his interest in the castle. In the public house many wild theories were proposed, each more preposterous than the last. He is an ancestor of the former lord of the castle and has returned to claim his throne, one man offered. Another said that he is a fortune hunter looking for hidden treasure on the castle grounds.

At last Galvin struck on the truth of the matter. The stranger was sent by the king to inspect the castle, to determine its viability to garrison the king's army.

This caused much commotion. Trent, who owned the general store, said over the uproar, "This is excellent lads. There will be an influx of visitors with coin to spend and more trade for our goods."

"Along with taxes!" someone countered.

"Imagine if the king garrisons an army here. All those men to trample our crops, bringing crime and violence," Galvin said.

"Armies bring plagues," the miller said darkly.

"What if we are attacked by the king's enemies? They will burn Bunwych to the ground!" Calvert said.

In a few hours the consensus was this: any interest by the outside world was dangerous, perhaps even catastrophic to the town.

"What are we to do about it lads?" Trent shouted.

"We should do nothing. Most likely the poor man will either be dead or have fled in terror by morning," said Galvin.

"And what if he doesn't?" the miller said.

"We will cross that bridge when we come to it," Galvin said.

At that moment the door to the tavern burst open with a

gust of wind. There was a storm coming. The distant rumble of thunder sounded along with brief flashes of light far off in the sky. The men said abrupt goodbyes and rushed to the safety of their homes. Those that had livestock brought their animals in for the night.

Galvin returned home and changed into his bedclothes. He took great pleasure in reading in bed for an hour or two each night. When he settled into his bed he became aware of the sound of many small feet, at least a dozen, pattering up above in the attic. Frowning, he opened his book and began to read. A few moments later fiddle music clamored from the attic, quite loud, either a jig or a reel, (he could never tell the difference). Presently the pattering of feet began to sound distinctly like dancing. He covered his ears with his pillows and tried to sleep.

By midnight the storm was upon Bunwych. A mighty clap of lightning struck a tree just beyond the castle causing Terrell to wake and sit up instantly, his heart pounding. It took a few moments for him to remember where he was. He sat up and drank some water. The hairs prickled on the back of his neck. He sensed another presence. Turning to the window he saw floating there an apparition. It looked like an old woman with a gaunt, almost skeletal face, its ghastly white hair billowed in the wind. Where its eyes should be there was just blackness, a dreadful void. Its mouth opened and there came the most hideous shrieks, of anguish or rage he could not tell, perhaps both. Terrell wanted desperately to cover his ears but he sensed that any display of fear would somehow prove fatal. Instead, he composed himself and walked towards the window boldly.

"Be gone banshee, this castle is mine now. I will not leave!" he shouted.

This only seemed to enrage the creature more and it shrieked even louder. Terrell defiantly pulled a chair up and sat grimly, watching the creature. After some time had passed, perhaps half or perhaps an hour, the thing abruptly stopped howling and floated back down to the ground. Terrell got up and watched it disappear through the front gate.

Somehow, he sensed it would not return, so went back to bed and slept soundly.

"Be gone banshee, this castle is mine now. I will not leave!" he shouted.

Three Days Before Midsummer's Eve

The next morning Galvin awoke to a commotion outside his room. Climbing up the ladder to the attic he saw not two but four goblins. After that there was much hammering, sawing, and stomping coming from above. Galvin dressed and stood at the ladder looking up into the attic.

"Say now, eh, Mr. Dozank..."

A moment later the goblin's head popped out from above. He said, "Good morning master. I trust you slept well?"

"Why, no actually I was awakened-" Galvin said.

"I took the liberty of asking my two cousins to help with the repairs of your roof which is decayed and leaking. That is satisfactory I hope?" Dozank interrupted.

"Well, I eh, suppose so," Galvin said. He felt tired and went to eat his breakfast.

Terrell awoke and explored the rest of the castle. He found a long hallway in the living chambers with paintings of the castle's past inhabitants. The (the what?) was a handsome lord of middle age, his attractive lady, a beautiful young lady, and several younger men and women which he guessed were the children.

He found a broom and with nothing else to do, began the monumental task of cleaning the derelict castle. In one storage room cluttered with junk, he found a chest containing some clothing. He pulled out a fine pair of trousers, incredibly still like new. Gathering a complete set of clothing, he went down to the river to wash and replace his tattered rags with these fine, though somewhat anachronistic vestments.

Julia awoke late in the morning troubled with frightening dreams of ghosts. She was going mad not knowing whether or not her knight lived or died. When her mother was out fetching milk, she quickly packed a basket of food and set off for the castle. Morris spotted her and ran after her.

"Where are you going?" he asked.

"I'm taking some food to someone in town. Go away," she said, irritated.

"I'll come with you. I want to see if the knight survived the night," he said.

"Of course he survived. He is a knight, isn't he?" she asked.

Seeing that she could not get rid of him she confided, "I'm taking the food to the knight, but you mustn't tell mother, alright?"

"Alright," he said eagerly.

Despite warnings from parents to stay away, children from town sometimes dared explore the ruined castle, though always in the daytime. Julia and Morris nervously passed through the gatehouse and into the grounds.

Terrell was just returning from his washing, smiled at the children and said, "Hello Lady Julia, is this your brother?"

"Yes, his name is Morris," she said.

There was an awkward silence, then she added, "My mother asked me to bring you some more food."

"That was very kind of her. But aren't you afraid of the ghosts?" he asked.

"No, it is safe in the daytime," Morris said.

"Yes, so it is. Well, will you two join me in my breakfast?" he asked.

Morris grinned and Julia said, "Yes, thank you."

They found a block of stone to serve as a table and spread

out the food on the towel which had covered the basket. Terrell told the children stories of court, although he declined to mention that he was a prince and heir to the throne. He prodded the children for more information about the castle and its origins but they knew nothing of value.

When they were finished he said, "Thank you for the meal and please send my thanks to your kind mother. Here." He took out a copper coin and gave it to Julia.

Julia was by this time quite in love with the dashing knight, and Morris, who had only ever known stooped old men or rough country lads, idolized the young man. His imagination was on fire with all of the stories he told.

Witches' Revenge

After Morris and Nessa ran away, the witches familiar – the giant spider, was able to open the oven door and free her. She was badly burned and even with her most powerful healing magic, weeks passed before she could leave the hut. For the entire time of her recovery, her only thought was of revenge but her prey had escaped. She knew what Nessa looked like, of course, but the girl was insignificant, and her familiar could not see the one who pushed her into the oven. She sensed magic was in play and magic was needed to combat it.

It was midnight on the night of the new moon and the clouds hid even the dim light of the stars. The witch was in a dank, swampy part of the forest near her hut. The only light came from a candle made from fat rendered down from the flesh of a hanged man. The candle was held by the hand and arm bones of a rival witch, killed by her many years ago.

She bent down to a small, dark green plant with long, pointed leaves. Using tongs fashioned from the bones of a murderer, she plucked three small, dark green berries and put them in a tiny clay flask, careful not to touch them.

She returned to her hut and added other ingredients to the flask; five drops of venom of an adder, some foam from the mouth of a rabid dog, and lastly, a few drops of her own urine.

Thereupon, she cut out a rectangular piece of vellum, made from the skin of a newborn. Using a quill made from a vulture feather, and using the concoction from the flask as ink, she drew intricate runes into the paper. She was now ready but she needed to wait to find out the identity of her enemy.

Meanwhile, Julia was practicing her own magic. When everyone was in bed, she got up and pretended that she needed to use the loo. Instead she picked three bay leaves from the plant which grew along the south side of the house and put them in her pocket. Next, she went to a bucket of water which she had prepared in the morning by throwing a bunch of red roses into it. Dipping her fingers in the pail, she sprinkled the bay leaves with the rose water. She returned to bed and put the leaves under her pillow. That night she dreamed of Sir Terrell, and so knew he was the one she would one day marry.

Terrell's Second Night – The Phantom Hound

That night Terrell lay down to sleep grimly prepared for another night such as before. At the strike of midnight his sleep was abruptly interrupted by a low bestial growl coming from the hallway. He opened his eyes and listened. Without further warning the beast was atop him, its jaws snapping for his throat. Just barely managing to get his hands up in time, he held the creature away. The lamp was out and the only light came from a half moon shining through the far window. The monster was black, shaped like a dog, but giant, bigger than the biggest mastiff. Its eyes glowed red like a glowing ember and it reeked of decomposing flesh.

Terrell was pinned down to the bed, not daring to let go and make a grab for his sword. With his strength beginning to fail he made a desperate move. With all his might he pushed up with his left hand while at the same time pulling down with his right. The monster flipped over and crashed to the floor. Not wasting an instant, Terrell went for his sword. He just managed to draw the sword when the beast was on him again. He blocked its bared fangs with the blade and kicked it away. This gave him just enough time to raise the sword for a blow.

The sword bit deeply into the creature's skull. Its red eyes flickered off like a candle being blown out and it sank to the floor without even a whimper. He turned to fetch the lantern to get a better look at the monster. When he turned back the creature was gone with not even a trace of blood.

He lay back on the bed to sleep but this time he kept his sword within reach.

Two Days Before Midsummer's Eve

The Blacksmith

Cedric, the village blacksmith, was renowned in the village as a morose, silent man. He had few friends and seldom came to the public house, spending virtually all his time at his home and his workshop which was a short walk from his house. His wife was long since dead and he had only one child, a daughter of 15 years, named Aldith. The townspeople knew of her, but few had ever seen her. The gossip was that she was touched – feeble minded, but no one really knew.

One fine spring day, when the air was full of the sweet scent of holly blossoms, Alec walked the lonely path to the blacksmith shop. He was sent by his mother to order some hinges for a door on their new barn. He came to the shop and saw that it was shuttered. Not wanting his long journey to be wasted, he continued on to the house of the blacksmith. Soon, he spied the small wooden cottage through the budding trees. He heard a snapping sound, as if someone were whipping an animal and he circled to the back of the house to see what was occurring.

What he saw caused the blood to freeze in his veins. A young woman; Aldith, was chained to a post and Cedric, her father, was whipping her. The rags she wore were torn and blood was soaking in from the wounds on her back.

After a few more lashes Cedric stopped and unfastened her from the post.

"Why do you make me do this?" Cedric said exasperated.

Then he dragged her into the house, pulling the chain attached to a bracelet on her ankle like a dog on a leash.

Alec dropped down to his knees, overcome with emotion.

When he saw the face of Aldith, he was thunderstruck. She was the most beautiful creature he had ever seen. Her dark hair and dark eyes bewitched him. He staggered home, his mind consumed with thoughts of revenge on the villain and how to free Aldith from her captor.

Alec had a sleepless night, his mind filled with Aldith. The next morning he was determined to do something to free the girl, but what he did not know. He wished he could ask his mother for help but feared she would order him to forget her and stay out of their business.

He returned to the blacksmith, still tasked with ordering the new hinges. This time Cedric was there in the forge working. Alec stood in the doorway for a few moments, watching him work, hate smoldering inside him. At last he found the courage to enter, walking beside the smith so that he could be seen.

Cedric noticed him and paused in his hammering. He said gruffly, "What do you need boy?"

"Two hinges for the barn door," Alec said, equally gruffly.

"Come back tomorrow," he said and resumed his work.

Alec headed for the house where Aldith would be found. The metallic hammer blows could still be heard, reassuring him that the smith was still in his forge.

The smith's house was the common one floor design with an attic space in the steep roof which usually served as the sleeping area. All of the shutters were closed. Alec spied a large branch and dragged it over to the house. He propped it up against the wall and easily scrambled up to the attic window. The shutter was closed but not locked and he easily pushed it open.

Inside he saw Aldith lying on a straw mattress. She was wearing a new dress, still mean but not as bad as the torn bloody rags of the previous day. She cowered in the corner, keeping away from the light streaming in.

For a few moments Alec couldn't speak, not knowing what to say. At last he said, "I want to help you escape."

This caused a transformation in Aldith. She relaxed and turned to look towards him. She said, "I am chained here and only my father has the key." She shook the chain attached to her ankle and pulled it against the loop securing it to the wall.

"Why does he treat you so?" Alec asked.

Her confidence growing, she looked directly at him and said, "He is wicked. He blames me for my mother's death."

Gallantry rose in Alec's heart and he said, "I will find a way to free you."

"Thank you! Thank you!" she said smiling.

Alec suddenly turned his head back outside. The hammering had ceased. "I will return tomorrow!" he whispered urgently.

He quickly slid back down the branch and dragged it back into the woods. Then he continued on, heading back home.

Terrell's Third Night – The Spectral King

The next morning he decided to go into town to buy some more provisions. The people he passed on the street looked surprised to see him. Whether this was because of the ancient clothes or because they were surprised that he still lived, he did not know.

He went into the shop. Trent was there stacking boxes and nearly fell off the ladder when he saw the knight enter. Terrell tried to engage him in conversation but Trent was reticent, though polite. He grabbed a few bottles of wine, a wheel of cheese, and a loaf of bread, paying with some more of his ancient coin.

As he was walking back to the castle he heard a man crying out for him. It was Galvin, walking quickly trying to catch up with the knight.

"Good afternoon," he said. His face was red and flushed from the exercise.

"Good day."

"Good sir knight, I couldn't help but notice you purchased some of our humble wine. Now, I could not allow a man of such noble bearing drink such common stock while a finer vintage lies in my cellar gathering dust."

"I'll wager your wine less humble and my nobility less exalted than you give me credit for, but I accept your offer." Terrell was eager for some conversation, and needed more information about the castle and the lands nearby.

"Excellent!" Galvin clapped his hands together joyfully.

The men turned and Terrell followed Galvin back into town.

As they neared Galvin's fine house Terrell noticed he became more nervous and would not look him in the eyes. Terrell wondered if he was unwise to have left his sword at the castle. Still, after defeating the Giant Galifron, Terrell felt like he could face a band of angry villagers.

"Excuse my sheepishness, it suddenly occurs to me that my house isn't exactly in a state suitable for visitors such as you," Galvin said as he began to back away from Terrell towards his house.

Terrell began to protest but Galvin held up his hands and rushed to his front door, saying "Just allow me one minute to straighten up!"

Terrell waited by the door, hearing an occasional crash of metal, scattered banging, the sound of furniture moving, and several hushed shouts of Galvin.

After some time Galvin reappeared in the doorway and said, "I am terribly sorry about that. Please come in."

Terrell entered and the room was indeed in a state. There were empty wine bottles everywhere, Some of the furniture was in bad repair, and there were several holes in the wall and ceiling.

"Please, sit down," Galvin said and motioned to a fine upholstered chair which looked like something had taken an enormous bite out of.

Galvin disappeared into another room and returned with a bottle and two glasses. With great pride he uncorked the bottle and poured two glasses.

The wine was good but Terrell of course had far better, although he did not mention that to his host.

"It is quite unusual to have a visitor of your stature come to our town," Galvin said. It was obvious to Terrell that he was fishing for information.

"Why is that? Your land is obviously fertile, you have a good, clean river, and a goodly castle although it is in disrepair."

"Oh. Well, I don't know. I suppose we are hard to reach,

far from any city," Galvin gulped down some wine, a bit too quickly, and started to cough.

"Yes, you certainly are hard to reach. Does the river flood often?"

"No," he answered immediately, then seemed to reconsider, "'Well, that is, yes, occasionally," Galvin stammered.

"How many acres of farmland surround the castle?"

"How many... acres? Oh, well, I don't think I know precisely."

"Is the town ever molested by bandits?"

"Bandits! Oh I should say not." Galvin looked quite disturbed at Terrell's hard line of questioning and Terrell began to feel sorry for the man.

Abandoning this tact, he said softly, "you are anxious that I will lead an army back here and destroy your beautiful peaceful town." By this time the two men had each finished two glasses of wine and were on their way through a third.

Galvin blinked and nodded, looking down.

"Don't you realize that if the king decides to restore this castle, it would be a boon for this town. You could become one of the greatest cities in the land. All of you founders would be wealthy."

Galvin did not answer. Terrell saw both great sadness and wisdom in Galvin's eyes and knew this man would not be swayed by promises of wealth or grandeur.

"Thank you for sharing your wine with me. It was excellent."

"Oh, no not at all. The honor was mine."

Terrell headed back to the castle and could not help but feel sorry for Galvin and the other townspeople. It was true; an army unleashed on this unspoiled country would be terrible, even if no battles occurred. A foraging army can lay bare a field of crops worse than a ravenous plague of locusts or rats. He had seen that himself even in his limited experience with war. He thought about Wyn and Julia and the other women in the village and what even disciplined soldiers were capable of. Shaking his head, he tried to put those thoughts out of his mind and focus on his duty to the king.

This, the third night, Terrell took the precaution of barricading his door with some scrap lumber. He kept the lamp on low all night and laid down to sleep. Sleep didn't come so easily this night but by midnight with the aid of more wine, he again fell into a light slumber.

He awakened suddenly and noticed a foul odor. He grasped the sword that lay on his chest. There in the room something was slowly materializing from a kind of dark smoke. He sat up, dread welling in his guts. It took the shape of a man, only it was twice as big as a man, black as pitch and with huge, bulging muscles. Like the banshee, its eyes were a black void. In a deep, resonant, unnatural voice it spoke, "Who dares inhabit my castle?"

"Forgive me, my lord, I thought the castle was uninhabited," Terrell replied as calmly as he could.

"It is not. And what's more you've slain my hound."

"Again I beg your pardon, but it attacked me in the night. I was compelled to defend myself," Terrell said.

"You are brave and courtly but still I must punish you," It said grimly and started to move towards him.

"How did you enter my room without opening the door?" Terrell said quickly, an idea forming in his mind.

The creature uttered a sound which was like a scoff and said, "That was nothing, I came in through the keyhole."

"What? That is not possible. You must have a key,"

Terrell now knew the creature's weakness; vanity.

"Not possible? You just watch!" it said.

The thing quickly dematerialized and passed back through the keyhole.

Terrell instantly jumped up, grabbed an empty bottle and placed the opening against the keyhole just as the vapor began to come back through. He waited until the creature was entirely inside the bottle then sealed the opening with the cork. The bottle was a tinted brown glass and he could not see inside, but he was glad of that. He placed the bottle in the corner and sat up against the wall, waiting for dawn, not daring to sleep.

One Day Before Midsummer's Eve

In inner Bunwych, near the village green, was a warehouse in which Mr. Horton stored barrels of apple juice. Morris and two friends picked the primitive lock easily and took one of the barrels. It was very heavy so they rolled it down the lane to one of the hedges surrounding the green and pushed it into the hedge and covered it with brush to hide it. With their task completed, they went to the river to swim.

Meanwhile, the adults were making their own less clandestine preparations; baking cookies, sweet breads, biscuits, puddings, and other treats for the children to take.

The Promise

Alec stood at the open doorway to the forge and watched the blacksmith work. Cedric took a white hot ingot out of the furnace and quickly placed it atop the anvil, then he grabbed his hammer and beat at it, sparks flying and falling to the stone floor like red snowflakes. Alec stepped inside where he could be seen and watched silently. The ingot's color changed to a dull gray and Cedric plunged it into a barrel of water with a sharp sizzle. Then he walked over to a table, picked up a pair of hinges and held them out to Alec.

"Two copper," he said.

Alec counted out two of the coins given to them by Terrell and held them out to Cedric. He took the coins and handed the hinges over. Alec saw the blacksmith's rippling muscles and wondered how he could defeat the man. He felt like a weak boy.

"Anything else?" Cedric asked, his brow narrowing.

Alec turned and left without replying. When he was a few paces away he could hear the blacksmith working again, and he turned toward Aldith's house. Finding the same branch as before, he climbed up to her window. She was sitting up on a chair looking into a small foggy mirror, brushing her hair. Alec watched her for a moment, his heart pounding. Not knowing what to say, he knocked on the window sill to make some noise.

She turned and smiled at Alec. "You came back!" she said.

"I said I would return," Alec said, encouraged that she was so glad to see him.

She came closer to Alec, until her chain stopped her a couple feet away.

"What is your name?" she asked.

"Alec."

"I am Aldith." Alec marveled at how friendly and unreserved she was despite the fact that she was a prisoner her entire life.

Alec couldn't think of a thing to say.

"Where do you live Alec?"

"In outer Bunwych, near the river."

"You are very brave to help me escape."

"Where does your father keep the key?"

"Around his neck. I think he even keeps it there when he sleeps."

Alec frowned and thought for a moment. "There must be a way to break the chain."

"No, brave Alec. The chain is enchanted. It cannot be broken."

"Then I will tell my mother. She will lead the town's men here and make your father free you."

She frowned at the boy and his heart nearly broke. "No! Do not tell anyone else. He will tell lies and they will take his side and then he will beat me, maybe even kill me." She turned and started to cry. Alec's heart felt as if it would break.

"Stop crying, please!"

"I thought you were brave," she said between sobs.

"I am, please tell me what I should do."

She stopped sobbing and turned back to him. She was almost smiling now. "You must sneak into the forge while he is working, take up a metal bar, and swing it at him with all your might."

Alec paled. "You mean kill him?"

"Yes, it is the only way. Will you free me, my brave boy?" she said, looking deep into his eyes.

"Yes."

"I knew you were the one. Now you must go before he finds you here. Alec, please hurry. He hurts me." He grew numb with fear and fury.

Alec slid back down the branch and put it back into the woods. He walked home, his mind reeling. He had never killed anything before. Even when he caught a rabbit he would persuade Nolan to kill it for him. Thinking of Nolan, and the worry he felt over Aldith made him morose.

He opened the cottage door and handed the hinge over to his mother. She looked at him strangely, for a moment he suspected she knew everything.

"Are you ill?" she asked, feeling his forehead.

"No."

"I will make you some tea," she said, disappearing into the hut doorway.

Alec returned to the reedy stream. "Wild man! Wild man! Wild man! I need you!" he called out.

In a few minutes the wild man appeared and beckoned for Alec to follow. He led him back to the campsite by the mountain side and sat down by the fire which was burning low. The wild man tended the fire silently. Alec waited to speak until he was asked.

"Why did you summon me?" he finally asked.

"I... I met a girl, the blacksmith's daughter. He is imprisoning her. She is chained like a dog. I promised to help her but the only way is to kill him and take the key from around his neck. I am afraid. I am not big enough to kill him."

The wild man stood and looked sadly at him.

A biting fly came and landed on Alec's forehead. Swift as the wind, Brogan swatted the fly with an open palm with enough force to knock Alec over and make him see stars.

He stood back up angrily, "Why did you do that?"

"The fly was harming you. I killed it for you."

Alec frowned and sat back down. There was a period of silence then Alec said softly, "I understand."

"Wait here." Brogan went into his cave and in a few moments returned with a metal file the length of his forearm.

"The file is enchanted. It will cut through the chain."

Without a word, Alec took the file and left.

He hid the file outside the house near the chicken coop and went inside. Tomorrow was Midsummer's Eve. Cedric would be at the village green celebrating with the other adults.

Morris Flies A Broom

Morris was in his tree house staring up at the clouds, bursting them apart with his mind. Sometimes he would do this for hours.

The notion came to him in a flash. He scrambled down the rope and ran straight home, then retraced the path he took home when he rescued his sister from the witch. At a certain part of the path, he slowed and carefully scanned the forest floor. After a few minutes of this he found what he was looking for; the witches' broom, which he discarded the other day without a second thought. The broom, he hoped, was magic, and would allow him to fly.

He placed the broom between his legs but nothing happened. He commanded it to fly, still nothing. Not giving up, he tried running with it, jumping off rocks with it, anything he could think of, he tried. Nothing worked.

Morris came to the lake and called out, "Swan Faerie!"

In about a minute she emerged in her humanoid form, walking out of the water. The water ran off her in beads.

She crouched down, smiling and embraced the boy. "You defeated the witch. I am so glad."

"I have her broom but I don't know how to fly with it. Can you help me?"

She became grave, "Burn the broom and anything else you found from the witches' hut. It is cursed."

"But I destroyed her and she can no longer harm anyone. Please tell me how to use it."

"You are stubborn and must learn for yourself, I see. Very well, hand me the broom."

She took it and held it in front of her for a moment. "The

spirit of the wood has told me the key to the magic. Command the broom to *eitil*, and it will obey."

Eagerly Morris took back the broom. He held it between his legs and said the magic word. The broom lurched forward so suddenly he almost lost his grip on it, but he managed to hang on. It was moving forward at a low angle and a row of thorns was directly in his way. He tilted the head of the broom up and it quickly rose up, lifting him above first the thorns, then the trees. Soon he was as high as the hawks soar and the trees below were like small green bushes. He could see the river far below, the town on one side, and the forest spreading out endlessly on the other. Instinctively, Morris knew he should keep his trinket secret, and so he flew away from the view of Bunwych, towards the forest. He tilted the broom down, going into a dive. The wind roared in his ears as he soared faster than a horse could run, faster than any boy had ever gone.

He flew for hours, not heeding hunger or thirst. Only when the sun began to set did he consider landing. Flying just above the trees, he landed in a small clearing near his house. Earlier in the summer, Morris built a lean-to hidden in a secluded cluster of boulders. Here he kept his magical hat of invisibility and any other bauble he wished to keep safe. He put the broom inside and rushed home.

The witch was in her hut brewing a potion which would allow her to divine the name of her attacker when she heard a crow outside calling to her. She rushed outside. It was startled and flew up, then back down again twenty feet away.

"What do you know?" she asked the crow in his own language.

"Reward!" It crowed.

The witch reddened with anger but went back inside the hut and grabbed a handful of grain. She tossed it at the crow which immediately began pecking at the scattered food.

"Tell me!" she said.

"We have seen your broom in the air," it said.

"Who rides it?"

"A human boy," it said, still eating the grain.

The bird was now only feet away and the witch pounced in it with surprising quickness. The crow struggled but she held it firm. Her eyes rolled back and she went into a trance. She now saw what the crow saw, knew what it knew. After a moment she smiled and released the bird, which flew off flustered and agitated.

The morning sun of early summer shone through deep green leaves and cascaded its dappled light onto the forest floor. The usual cacophony of birdsong was muted this morning and the breeze was oddly still but Morris paid no heed. His mind was on other things.

An old woman slowly shambled down the narrow footpath into Bunwych. She struggled to carry a bundle of firewood and had to stop every few minutes to rest. A small black pup trotted at her side. Morris emerged from a side path. He was heading towards the river to meet his friends for a morning swim. He saw the old woman and was surprised to not know her or her dog, for he knew every living creature in Bunwych, or thought he did. She was now breathing heavily and looked quite pathetic.

"Please, may I carry your bundle for you?" he said.

"Thank you. You are very kind."

She handed over the bundle which was tied together by twine, to Morris who found it quite light. He turned and started walking in the direction she was heading when he heard a hideous cackling. He swung around and standing there was the witch and her giant spider. She was grinning triumphantly.

He dropped the firewood, along with the rune inscribed paper which was hidden inside, and staggered back.

"The curse is accepted, and so mote it be!" she spit out.

Morris turned and ran, and although the witch did not give chase, her cackling seemed to him to breathe down his back until he reached the house. He went straight up to his bed, ignoring his mother's questions.

Wyn's medical skills were unsurpassed in the village. In fact, the children were seldom sick and when they started to feel unwell she would always know the right salve, philter, or potion to set them right. She was often sought out by others in the village to nurse a sick loved one; a responsibility she would take on reluctantly.

She felt Morris' forehead. There was a slight fever, so she gave him some willow bark tea.

"Don't look so worried. You'll be back on your feet soon enough," she told him. *It's not like him to be so dispirited from a fever,* she thought. A dark cloud of intuition passed over her for a moment, but she cast it aside.

It was so cold that the dwarfs could see their breath freeze in the air. The cavern was so big it was not possible to see the edges in the dim torch light.

The Third Task – Chop Down a Tree With Water

The way to the Gelid Chasm was through a remote part of the dwarf underworld that had long since abandoned. Millennium ago, dwarf miners seeking gold broke through the rock revealing an immense chamber. Explorers were lowered. Faint screams were heard far, far below. The ropes were raised and up came the explorers, frozen solid and encrusted with ice. That could only only mean one thing; ice drakes. A sturdy door was installed to keep out the perilous creatures and the shaft has remained abandoned ever since.

Gomrund, Arngrim, and ten of the king's stoutest guards were now at that door. It was rusted closed and took them the better part of an hour to open. A pulley and rope were constructed above the chasm and the first dwarf was lowered. He reached the bottom and the rope loosened. No cries of agony were heard. It was hauled back up and the next dwarf went down, then another. Finally the king was lowered. A crew remained up at the top to raise them back up.

It was so cold that the dwarfs could see their breath freeze in the air. The cavern was so big it was not possible to see the edges in the dim torch light. A faint but steady sound of dripping could be heard as water dripped down from high above. Stalactites rose up far above their heads like small mountains. They picked a path between them, moving slowly and silently across patches of black ice. Occasional strange noises could be heard but they could not determine any direction because of the echoes. Suddenly there was a hissing sound and one of the men gasped. The group turned, and the man in the rear was frozen solid, still standing. Ice crystals glistened on his skin and a small icicle dangled down from his nose. The group turned; standing calmly in a crack between two rocks was an ice drake. It was blue-white in color, and looked like a common salamander except it was three feet from head to tail. It's eyes were pure white. One of the guards with a torch thrust it out towards the drake and it quickly turned and disappeared.

"After it!" commanded Gomrund.

The men obeyed and the king followed in the rear. They ran for several minutes, the dwarf in the lead calling out encouragingly.

"We have it cornered," shouted the lead dwarf.

Gomrund pushed through the guards. The drake was indeed cornered in a dead end. It wheeled and breathed. A mass of white frost billowed out. The dwarfs dove for cover but one was too slow and was instantly frozen solid. The others quickly formed a perimeter around the beast, keeping the two torch carriers between them and the drake.

"Quickly! Set up the cage!" Gomrund commanded.

Two of the dwarfs took materials they were carrying and quickly reassembled them into a wooden box reinforced with iron bars. A hinged door was on one end of the box. They then pushed the box towards the creature.

Gomrund cleared his throat, and in an ancient language known only to the dwarf kings and their advisers, commanded the drake to enter the box, telling it that it will be returned when its task is complete. Slowly, reluctantly, the creature walked into the box.

They quickly closed and locked the door. Two dwarfs picked up the box and the group headed back to the entrance.

The dwarf king had sent word that the third and final challenge will be performed on this day at noon. Tomos, Catrin, Galvin, and half of the village gathered at the village green, eager to see how the king would achieve this challenge. Few at this time doubted he would.

At exactly noon, the dwarf entourage arrived. There was

the king and Arngrim at the lead. Behind them were a contingent of six dwarf soldiers bearing what at first appeared to be a coffin. Behind those dwarfs were two other older dwarfs who were not in uniform. They bore another, smaller wooden box.

With much formality and ritual, Arngrim unrolled the marriage document and read from it. "Gomrund the Magnificent, King of all the Dwarfs, slayer of giants, and lord of the caverns will now perform the third and final challenge as inscribed in the contract, the groom must fell a tree with nothing but water."

Angrim lowered the scroll and looked about, focusing on a stout but average sized beech tree at the edge of the green, and said, "That tree there will suffice, will it not?"

Galvin stepped forward and said, "I think it fitting that the bride's father select the tree, would it not?"

Arngrim lowered his gaze and peered at the old man who was almost as short as he. "The contract does not specify a tree, therefore, any average tree will be adequate."

Galvin colored slightly and lowered his head, staring at his shoes.

The crowd formed a circle around the tree and watched as the smaller box was placed on the ground and its top removed, to reveal what appeared to be a bed of clay with an impression in it.

"Please fetch us a bucket of water," said Arngrim.

The water was brought and one of the dwarfs grabbed it and poured it into the clay mold. The larger box was placed in front of the mold.

"For your own safety, please keep back," Arngrim commanded to the human crowd, which murmured nervously and took several steps back.

From one end of the box, a soldier pulled a chain attached to the other end causing it to open. For a count of three heartbeats nothing happened, when suddenly there was a hiss and a cloud of billowing frost ushered from the box and enveloped the clay mold. In a moment the cloud had cleared revealing the mold covered with a sheet of frost. Two of the dwarf engineers disassembled the box, and freed the ice from the mold, holding up a crystal clear ax made of nothing but ice. They wrapped a leather cloth around the handle and handed it to the king. The king smiled slightly and held up the ax and began his work. The ax bit deeply into the trunk and in a few minutes was nearly half way through the trunk. The engineer stepped up and took the ax from the king which was now dripping water and placed it on the ground in front of the cage. Once again the end was opened and the drake did his duty and refroze the ax. Soon the king resumed chopping. At last he took one last stroke and paused. The tree gave a loud crack, and began to topple. The crowd had to scramble to move out of the way. Many of the villagers shouted out a cheer at the impressive display, but Tomos and Galvin were grim faced.

Arngrim said, "A clerk will be sent later today to work out the details of the ceremony."

With that, the dwarf entourage quickly and efficiently packed up and left.

The False Bride

That evening Tomos paced to and fro along the floorboards, his forehead knitted with concern.

"I have an idea!" exclaimed Galvin.

The village green was splendid. The hawthorns which encircled the park were in full bloom, their pink flowers glowing in the morning sunlight. Garlands of wildflowers hung from strings which were strung from tree to tree; sky-blue bluebells, golden primroses, purple foxgloves, and the blood-red mountain garland. As was the custom in Bunwych, all the village children went out in the morning and gathered as many wild flowers they could find. The child who brought the most flowers wins a prize from the bride's mother, usually a sweet cake. On these occasions, many a town flower bed was raided.

King Gomrund's party had arrived. It was just he and his adviser Arngrim. The king had a sour look on his face. He detested weddings, and especially his own. He wanted a simple Dwarf ceremony but Arngrim argued that a royal wedding required a measure of pomp and circumstance and reluctantly he agreed.

Meanwhile, in the house of Tomos and Katrin, preparations were being made. Lyneth was dressed in a fine white gown. She enjoyed this, although in truth she did not fully understand the magnitude of the situation. At one hour before noon Galvin arrived dressed in a fine black suit. Tomos opened the door and the men nodded to each other grimly. Katrin led Lyneth down and the quartet solemnly made the march to the town green. Villagers watched and waved at the bride as she passed through town.

When they were in front of Galvin's house Tomos looked at and then poked his daughter. She scowled at him then a few seconds later, remembered the plan and feigned a faint.

"The bride has fainted! Bring her into my house," Galvin called out.

This they did. The parlor was empty of goblins as was prearranged. Katrin kept watch through the window at the dwarfs who waited impatiently.

"Dozank!" Galvin cried.

In an instant the goblin appeared, grinning.

"The bride is lovely," he said.

"Never mind that. Get on with it," Tomos said irritably.

Dozank scowled and said, "Have you the toad?"

Galvin picked up a box on the floor and uncovered it. Inside there sat a large, fat, ugly toad.

Dozank jumped up on a table and abruptly took out a slender knife. Katrin gasped. The goblin grinned then deftly cut off a lock of Lyneth's hair. He spit on it then lay it atop the toad. In a language none in the room had ever heard he invoked the spell.

There was a loud pop and a gust of noxious smoke and then suddenly there were two brides standing in the room, each completely identical to the other.

Lyneth was told to sit and wait there while the false Lyneth was led back outside. To Galvin and Tomos' relief, the dwarfs suspected nothing. On they continued to the village green where almost everyone in the town was already gathered.

And so the ceremony began. Arngrim read from the contract. The curate murmured some lines Gomrund irritably repeated.

The curate then turned to Lyneth and said, "Do you so consent?"

The false bride merely stood there and stared.

Tomos whispered to her, "Say yes darling... Just say yes."

A few more seconds passed then Lyneth opened her mouth and out came a croak.

King Gomrund stared in shock. Arngrim turned to him and whispered something to him urgently. The king turned and with a fierce scowl, uttered an incantation. There was a loud pop and a cloud of smoke, and where Lyneth stood, was once again the fat, ugly toad which quickly hopped away.

The king's eyes flared red and he spoke in his most commanding voice, "People of Bunwych, for this act of treachery, on this day each year henceforth, all of you that live in the town will be transformed into a toad and remain that way for a month!"

Angrim's eyes widened and he whispered urgent pleas to the king.

"Remain that way until sunset." With a hundred pops and a hundred puffs of smoke every human that was within the town walls was transformed into a large, fat, toad.

"Tomorrow I shall return, and if there is further treachery you will spend the rest of eternity as snails!"

The king and Arngrim stormed off.

The children took the opportunity to enjoy the experience of hopping and swallowing bugs. The adults, not knowing how to behave as toads, more or less just stood still. Old man Rawlins had the misfortune of being eaten by a snake. At exactly sunset the spell wore off and all was as it was. Even Rawlins emerged unharmed from the snake's stomach, the snake however, did not fare so well.

Terrell's Fourth Night – The Ghostly Queen

In the morning Terrell went into town and purchased a shovel. A pack of seven children began following him as he left the storehouse and peppered him with questions. This he tolerated gracefully but when they reached the castle he minded his solemn task and ordered them to be gone. He found a spot in the forest outside the castle walls and dug a hole six feet deep. There he buried the bottle which contained the phantasm, where he hoped it would stay for eternity.

As he walked back to the castle he spied Julia and Nessa passing through the gatehouse. He smiled and waved. Nessa grinned and broke into a run. This upset Julia who knew it was unladylike to run.

"We're sorry we didn't come yesterday, our mother wouldn't let us," Nessa said.

In truth, Nessa broke her promise of keeping their previous journey a secret, gushing out to Alec the stories Terrell had told them as soon as they returned. Wyn overheard these and forbade them to return. Only constant pleading by the children finally convinced her to let them return today.

"It's no matter, Nessa. I am glad to see you today," Terrell replied.

"Hello Lady Julia," he said.

She blushed and smiled.

"Where is Morris?" he asked.

"He is in bed with a fever," Julia replied.

Terrell was concerned. "I am sorry to hear that. I hope he recovers soon."

"He will. Our mother is a great healer," said Julia.

They ate the breakfast the children brought on the grass by

the river and Terrell told them stories about the king and life at court.

When it was time for them to return home Nessa said, "Sir Terrell, will you please walk us back home?"

"Nessa!" Julia scolded.

"She is afraid of the bulls," Julia explained, somewhat embarrassed.

"I would be honored to escort you home."

They walked past the orchards to the bull pasture.

"Walk between me and the bulls please," Nessa instructed.

"As you wish my lady," Terrell said.

"We must walk swiftly but not fast," she explained.

"Stop!" she cried dramatically, stopping and pulling a briar out of her bare foot.

Julia ignored her and walked on but Terrell obediently obeyed.

They resumed walking and neared one of the bulls.

"Don't look at it. Don't look it in the eye!" she exclaimed in a hushed voice, walking faster.

The bull meanwhile completely ignored the travelers and chewed some grass.

They were now past the pasture in the town proper.

"We are safe. You can go back now. Goodbye!" she said abruptly and ran off, catching up with Julia who turned and waved goodbye to Terrell.

Terrell waved and headed back to the castle.

On the fourth night Terrell didn't sleep. He was weary and

dreaded what terrible ghost this midnight would bring.

At midnight a woman seemed to step through the wall and stood at his bedside. She was wearing a long, white nightgown which flowed down to the floor. Her long hair was jet black and her complexion pale as parchment. She was the most beautiful woman he had ever seen but he sensed evil. He grabbed for his sword, but she said in a sweet but cold voice, "Please my Lord, help me."

His head reeled, he felt drunk, madly in love. He knew he was bewitched but he didn't care.

She sat down on the bed and they kissed passionately. He began to pull off her nightgown but then her slipper fell off and he saw her foot. Her left foot was green, four toed, and clawed, like some kind of lizard. Instantly the spell was broken. He threw her to the floor and raised his sword to strike. Before he struck the blow, she dematerialized without a trace.

Midsummer's Eve (day)

Liam reread the final entry and closed the book. His heart ached for Maeraddyth. He knew she was gone but never guessed the sacrifice she had made for him. Remembering her instructions, he walked over to a shelf and pulled down a small chest. Inside were some small rolls of yarn and thread of multiple colors, and a silver pair of scissors. He picked them up and admired the shiny, cold metal for a moment then put it in his pocket. Next he cast his invisibility spell and left the place that was his only haven for the last time. Quietly he followed the exact path Maeraddyth described in the book, leaving the goblin village and passing into the domain of the elves. He was careful to stop and wait quietly whenever he heard someone approach.

As he passed along a hedge which divided two meadows he heard horses approaching and ducked down as low as he could. They came closer and soon the two horses were standing right beside him, almost close enough to touch. He couldn't see their faces and hoped they couldn't see him either.

A male elf spoke, "Care to chase a hare?"

A female replied, "That would be delightful."

"I will ride down the hedge and scare one off," the man replied.

The man rode off quickly while the lady waited for a few moments, then, quite suddenly the horse and rider vanished and a fox was there in its place. Instantly, it took off running. Liam moved and was able to see the fox running off in the opposite direction, no doubt in pursuit of a hare.

Liam didn't hesitate and ran across the field. The grass was so tall it wrapped around his legs with every step he took and he ran more slowly than he would have liked.

On the other side of the field was a stand of trees. He was now on the edge of Elfhame, the human world was only feet away. He could already feel the tugging, the enchantment which prevented him from leaving. Following Maeraddyth's instructions to the smallest detail, he took out the silver scissors and cut in the air with them, two inches from his body, level with his navel. He fell backwards, as if he were leaning into a stiff wind that suddenly ceased. The spell was broken.

He turned and ran, not looking back. He knew roughly where to go. Maeraddyth drew a map of the village and where his family's hut was.

Alec grabbed the file and headed for Aldith's house, his heart pounding. He climbed up the branch to her window. She was there, waiting for him. He climbed inside and took the file out from his pocket and was about to explain when she said, "You promised!"

"This is a special file. It will cut through the chain!" Alec explained.

"He will find me and take me back. You must kill him. It is the only way I can be free."

She kissed him. His head reeled. He would do as she said. He would do anything for her.

"You will kill him?" she asked softly.

"Yes."

Alec climbed back down the branch and walked to the forge. As he suspected, it was empty. Cedric was no doubt at the celebration. The door was unlocked and Alec crept in. He found a stout iron rod and felt it in his hand. He grabbed a bucket and sat in the dark by the door, waiting.

An hour before dusk, Alec heard footsteps outside. He felt trapped. He stood on top of the bucket and readied the weapon.

The door creaked open and a man stepped inside. It was too dark to see but Alex knew it was the blacksmith. Feeling trapped, like an animal that must kill or be killed, Alec swung down with the pipe as hard as he could. There was a dull bell-like sound as the rod crashed against Cedric's head. He crumpled to the floor, facing down, blood flowing from his wound. Alec felt a terrible gnawing in his heart, a sense of guiltiness even worse than when Nolan was killed by the Ogre because this time he killed Cedric himself. Yet there was also an exultation, because he had done the right thing to free Aldith. He grabbed the key from Cedric's belt and rushed back to Aldith.

He showed her the key.

"You must do it," she said.

Alec bent down and inserted the small key in the lock. It turned easily and the shackle fell off her ankle.

She turned to Alec and took his hand. "Free! I am free. Take me to the river! Let's run!"

Still holding hands they ran, both laughing the whole time. She was fast. He could barely keep up with her. They reached the orchard near the river. The bare grassland sloped down and into the river, and there they sat, watching the water bubble over the rocks. The sun was almost set. Alec grabbed her shoulders, a little roughly and pushed her down, kissing her passionately. At first she responded, then pushed him off.

"I am sorry," Alec said.

She looked pale. "It's not that. I am hungry is all."

"There are ripe berries by the river." He quickly got up, eager to please her.

"No, I need meat."

"Let's go to the village green. There will be food there."

The sun was now set and the moon began to rise up just over the tree line.

She clutched at her stomach and bent down, moaning in pain.

"Aldith! What ails you?"

She collapsed to the ground, her pupils were huge, and her face was a strange ruddy color.

"You must go! Run!"

"I will run and find help," he said, hesitating.

"Make haste!"

As fast as he could he ran back to his hut. His mother would know what to do.

Midsummer's Eve (night)

The Faerie Ball

The sun was setting. At last the night had come.

Julia waited until her mother was up stairs caring for Morris before leaving. She had hidden the dress in the barn the night before and now fetched it, folding it carefully into a knapsack. Next she fetched Nessa and together they went to join the rest of the children and wait for the time of the Faerie Ball.

False Liam never cared much for the midsummer games. He usually would skulk off on his own, finding a turtle to molest or a baby pig to steal and eat, or commit some other act of malicious intent. But this eve he was nearly fourteen, and he felt odd, there was a hotness in his blood that made him anxious, restless. He never felt like he belonged in this family. The humans seemed so alien to him, but what maddened him was he did not know why, for he never suspected that he was a changeling.

His sisters were shocked when he agreed to go with them to the celebrations. They left their house at dusk laden with cookies and cider and headed for the village green to join the other children.

By now it was dark and most of the village children were gathered in the village green. They were all chattering excitedly and feasting on the victuals. Elinor was the eldest child and so began the rituals. They started a bonfire, and began throwing sage leaves into it and taking turns jumping over the fire. There was a maypole and some of the younger children began to dance around it while singing an ancient rhyme. The older girls sat around the fire and prepared little discs of bread made out of flour and water. Into the dough they inscribed their names then cooked the bread over the fire using a stick. The cooked discs would then be collected and hidden in a large haystack. The older boys then gathered some distance away from the haystack and on the eldest boy's command, raced for the haystack where they would hunt for the discs of bread. Of course, if the boy wasn't happy with his prize, he could discard it and keep looking. In the end, each boy was expected to present the disc to its creator and the pair would go off together.

Midsummer's Eve

The children who knew how to play music played their recorders, fiddles, drums, accordions, and lutes. Attracted by the music, scores of pixies began to arrive, fluttering down from high above and joining in the revels with the children, whom they loved. Certain pixies began to play their own music while others entertained the children with displays of light magic. The warm, moist air was heavy with magic and the youths seemed to enter a state of almost religious fervor. The younger children, with arched backs, plump bellies, rosy cheeks, and berry stained lips stared with wide iris' into the night sky. The older ones, straight and lean with earnest furrowed eyebrows, began singing ancient songs handed down from sibling to sibling.

Alec reached the cottage and found his mother upstairs, tending to Morris.

"Mother! You must come. Cedric has a daughter and she is very sick. She is in the orchard by the river."

"Your brother is also very sick," she replied.

"Please Mother!"

Wyn came down the stairs and stood before Alec. "You love her," she said, half in teasing, half in admiration. For the first time he seemed like a man to her.

"Yes! Please hurry!"

They rushed to the orchard, on the way Alec telling her the full story of what happened, convinced in his mind that he had done the right thing. Wyn however, was not convinced, feeling that part of the story was missing.

When they reached the spot, Aldith was nowhere to be found.

"She must have recovered and returned home. Which is what we should do now, come."

"No, I must look for her," he said and ran off.

"Alec!" She called, but he didn't stop.

For Julia, the midsummer games seemed childish and held no allure for her this year. Without a word to anyone, she picked up her satchel and left the village green, heading south and passing over the faerie bridge. She followed the worn footpath leading toward the Dawns Maidens. At a clear and wide part of the path she stopped, and under the bright moonlight, stripped off her clothes, then took out the dress and pulled it over her. She fretted bitterly that she didn't have a mirror to make sure her hair was tolerable. Then she put her old clothes back in the satchel, and hid it next to the trail by a crooked old tree that she could not miss.

Julia passed over a hill and the forest abruptly ended, giving way to rolling green hills. She was almost there. As she passed over another hill the stones of the Dawn Maidens rose up into view. She could see the lights and hear people talking and laughing. A terrible wave of fear rushed over her. She felt alone and lost. For a moment she considered turning back when two elven maidens appeared. They were about Julia's height and looked her age, although in reality, since faeries aged so much slower, were much older. They wore bright yellow gowns which fell just above their knees.

"Come. We have been waiting for you," they said in unison and gently took her by the hand.

Dawn's Maidens was a group of thirteen standing stones formed in a circle. They were more ancient than the eldest faerie and the most sacred place in Elfhame. In the field beyond the stones were numerous open tents made of a rainbow of brightly colored fabrics which shimmered in the gentle summer wind. Hundreds of faerie lights hung magically in the air glowing like giant fireflies.

There were great crowds of faeries of both sexes, all of whom looked young and beautiful and were splendidly dressed. Many smiled and greeted her as she passed. She felt quite welcome and her fear melted away.

The two elfin maidens, who were named Moonweather and Moonglamaer, led Julia into a tent and began tending to her, putting up her hair and applying sparkling makeup to her eyes, giggling all the while.

"Now you are ready for the ball," they proclaimed and led her to an area where people were dancing.

Rollicking music filled the air although Julia could see no musicians. Scores of couples whirled around on the bare grass, completely uninhibited and dancing like wild beasts. Moonweather and Moonglamaer each took one hand of Julia's and they began to dance, teaching her the moves. As she danced Julia experienced an intoxicating sense of freedom and had the sensation that this was the place she was meant to be and dancing was what she was meant to do. The music continued, never stopping or slowing in tempo.

After a few dances Julia was out of breath and her friends led her over to another tent with tables of food and drinks. On the tables were fruit of every kind Julia knew and many she had never seen, all at the peak of ripeness and sweetness. Julia sampled many and felt energy restored to her. In fact, she felt intoxicated. A goblin, dressed in a shabby gray tunic and eyes downcast, entered the tent carrying a tray filled with drinks. Moonweather stuck out her slender foot, tripping the lowly servant as he left the tent. He stumbled forward and a tray full of empty crystal glasses were launched into the air, landing intact on the soft grass. In a desperate frenzy he began loading the glasses back on the tray. The faeries laughed gustily but Julia felt so sorry for the creature that she bent down to help him. For a moment the goblin looked her in the eyes with a look of terror in his face. He left and Julia looked up to see the faeries looking down at her with a frown.

A young male elf entered the tent and Moonweather and Moonglamaer ran off, laughing and looking back at them.

He saw Julia and smiled and said, "Dance with me."

He wore a navy blue tunic and dark blue leggings and was very handsome. He took Julia by the hand and led her back to the dancing. He made many funny remarks, sometimes making fun at other couples by imitating how others were dancing.

Suddenly his ever present grin vanished as he saw something behind Julia. He bowed and backed away. Turning, Julia saw before her the faerie queen.

She was beautiful; tall, slightly older than most of the other faeries, though still youthful looking. She wore the most grand of all the gowns in shimmering gold. She wore a gold crown on her head with brightly sparkling jewels.

She smiled and said, "Julia, I am so glad you are here."

Julia curtsied and blushed, not knowing what to say.

"Come, walk with me. You must be wondering why you have been invited here." She took Julia by the hand and led her to a more secluded area."

"Yes, my queen."

"I have a special interest in you. You see, your mother is my daughter. You are my granddaughter."

Julia's eyes widened and she nearly stumbled.

"You had no idea, did you? Your mother has kept many things from you for far too long. She and I were very close once. But then she met a man, a human, and came under his spell. I beseeched her to give him leave. I warned her that he was untrue but she was stubborn. She left Elfhame and married him, living as a human peasant. I think she did it to spite me, you know." She let out a dramatic sigh. "Soon, as I predicted, he tired of her and wandered off, leaving her alone with four children. She blamed me for breaking them apart and remained away out of spite, although I begged her to return. She prevented me from even seeing you children, but now you are of the age to make your own decisions.

"Take this mirror." A silver hand mirror materialized and she handed it to Julia. "Whenever you want to speak to me, use this. But keep it secret from your mother. She has lived amongst the humans for so long, eating their food, that she has lost her magic. She will be jealous of you, for you are just coming into your magic. Perhaps when you are a little older you can return and live here where you belong. Would you like that, Julia?"

"Oh, yes Your Majesty. I would like that very much."

"Good." The queen touched her lightly on the head and walked off.

Julia returned to the dancing and looked for the boy she was dancing with. After a little while she found him, but he was dancing with another faerie girl. She saw Moonweather and said hi, but she looked right through her. She felt awkward again, like she didn't belong. She realized sunrise would be soon. If she didn't make it home before sunrise her mother would be suspicious.

False Liam watched from the edge of the green with distaste. He hated pixies and soon tired of the events. He sullenly wandered off to the river. Some of the children became overheated and ran for the river to bathe. Liam saw them coming and hid in the shadows. He watched them pass then stood up to follow when Fiona, a little one of five, ran up to him and said, "Please take me to the river."

He hesitated for a moment then took her hand. He led her to the river away from the other children and they waded in. He sank down to his neck and floated while Fiona was happily splashing and singing. Something came over him and he became like an animal, and the girl his prey. She was like a squeaking mouse and he the stalking cat. Grabbing her by the shoulders, he shoved her down into the water. She struggled but was far too weak to resist. A few seconds passed but then something struck him on the head and he was stunned and let go of the girl. False Liam turned and to his amazement saw a boy that looked just like him. True Liam struck again, bloodying his lip. He tried to run but Liam grabbed him around the neck. False Liam broke free and grabbed a stick protruding from the bank and stabbed Liam savagely in the cheek, bloodying him. Liam punched him in the nose, and False Liam scrambled up the bank to flee. Liam followed, and now out of the water, was free to cast a spell with his hands. He cast a simple sleep spell which Maeraedeth had taught him years ago, and False Liam fell to the ground in a stupor.

After escaping Elfhame, true Liam had headed for Bunwych. He saw the children gathering at the village green and watched, keeping in the shadows. He searched the crowd for the one who took his place and finally spotted him. It was not hard, because he had lived in Elfhame for so long and eaten faerie food all his life, Liam had faerie sight, and was immune to the magic which made False Liam appear human. Liam watched him skulk off and followed. He was watching the entire time he attacked Fiona and sprang into action as soon as he realized what was happening.

True Liam looked up to see dozens of children watching him silently with horror. Fiona broke the silence, calling out, "it was him, the one in white!"

Like the other children, False Liam was clothed all in white, while True Liam still had his dingy brown goblin rags on. The crowd gasped as someone turned him over, revealing his face.

"It's Liam!" Elinor gasped. Then she looked at True Liam. "But you also look like my brother."

"This creature is a goblin, enchanted to look like me. I was stolen from my family after I was born, and made to live with the goblins."

The older boys rushed to the goblin and picked him up roughly.

One of the traditional games of Midsummer's Eve was called Wolves and Sheep. By drawing straws ten of the children are selected to be the wolves, the rest are the sheep. The sheep gather at the East Bridge and the wolves hide somewhere between the bridge and the Great Tree. The game starts and the sheep must make it to the great tree without being touched by a wolf. If a wolf does tag someone, they become a wolf as well. If a sheep meets a player they may say, "Wool or Creep, Wolf or Sheep?" and the player must stop and answer truthfully.

Nessa was playing, and being fast for her age, made to the tree first and watched while the others ran.

Suddenly, a real wolf appeared from the hedges. It was not huge, but its red eyes and snarling mouth gave it a terrible appearance. Another child saw the wolf and screamed. The racing wolf slammed into Nessa, taking her down, and began tearing at her.

Morris slept peacefully in his bed. Wyn sat quietly in the chair, sipping at some tea, never taking her eyes off Morris. She was puzzled that her remedies had not yet cured him, but confident that in the morning he would be again in full vigor. She would keep vigil all night.

Glancing at the spoons as she went to bed she noticed that Nessa's silver was tarnished dark red. She stood there for three heartbeats, her eyes widening in terror, her blood turning to ice. Then she flew out the door.

Unlike the witch, Wyn did not need a magical broom to fly. She flew so fast that anyone she passed saw only a rustling of the leaves and felt a rush of air brush by.

Alec felt her pass over him as she flew but could never guess it was his mother, thinking instead it was a very fast owl or bat.

The wolf was momentarily warded off Nessa by a swarm

of pixies, but these were as bugs to the wolf and it crouched for a second attack. Just as it was about to spring, Wyn landed in the field and thrust her right hand toward the wolf. An invisible wave of force shot from her hand at the beast, rustling the grass as it passed as fast as the wind. The wolf was hit and knocked twenty feet away from the bloody Nessa.

Rage in her eyes, she motioned like she drew a sword from a scabbard and a razor thin blade appeared in her hand shining brightly in the moonlight. She walked with quick strides to the stunned wolf and raised the blade to strike.

"No!" shouted a voice. It was Cedric. He ran between Wyn and the wolf which was lying on the ground stunned, with blood coming out of its snout. "It is my daughter. She is bewitched! Spare her! I beg you!"

Wyn glared at Cedric for a moment then the rage cleared from her eyes and she was a human mother again. She lowered the sword and turned away from the wolf. Almost instantly, a web of roots sprouted from the ground and grew over the wolf, trapping it. She ran to her daughter. Nessa was unconscious and her white dress was completely red with her blood. Two older girls were there holding cloths to her wounds.

Brent, keeper of the bell tower, arrived and pulled the rope which should have swung the heavy bell, but instead of the tolling of the bell, he heard the loud and plaintive baa of a sheep. Puzzled, he pulled again harder. Again the sheep cried but no bell. Finally realizing that this was a midsummer's night prank, he raced up the spiral staircase up to the bell, cursing all the while. As he expected, the rope was disconnected from the bell and instead tied to the tail of a sheep which had been brought up to the tower. He untied the beleaguered sheep and rang the bell five times in a row, indicating an unspecified danger to the town.

Word had already reached the parents about the incident at the river and almost everyone in town was congregated at the village green. The games were canceled early and the children were all sent home.

Wyn had returned home with Nessa and was tending to her terrible wounds. Aldith was still a wolf and still imprisoned in the cell of roots, and also guarded by three villagers who were armed with spears. False Liam, now a goblin, was locked up in a cell beneath the bell tower. Gathered in the crowded ale house were many of the townsmen. All were silent. The only sound was Kenhelm's asthmatic breathing.

Cedric sat in the center of the room, his eyes downcast and red with tears. Cedric began, "It happened fourteen years ago, almost to the day. I was a young man then, just married to Nolwen that spring. We were living in the old house just outside Bunwych proper, near the mill. We just gone to bed when I heard a terrible racket from the forest, like a great monster was crashing through the brush and shouting out bellows that were terrible to behold. I ran to get my spear and went outside. It was fifteen feet high and had a face like an ogre but only had one eye. The eye was bleeding and it had its arms out and staggering like it was blind. It just nearly missed my cottage, but was heading straight for Bunwych. I ran after it and threw the spear. I hit it in the back and it went mad with rage, spinning around and bellowing even louder. The spear fell and I picked it up and threw it again. This time I hit it in the neck and blood was coming out fast. It changed direction and ran off away from town. I ran after it, I didn't want it coming back." He said this defensively, as if he thought what he did was a crime.

"I chased it for a bit then it fell down and stopped moving. Then all a sudden, this old hag appeared in front of it. She was crying and fussing over it and muttering that it was her son. The thing was dead so I went back home. The next day I came back and the corpse of the monster was gone. I thought the matter ended but then that night the witch came to my house. The door slammed open all on its own and the witch came in. She said she cursed me and that I would know what it was like to lose a loved one."

"Well, nothing happened, not right away anyway. Nolwen had a baby, our Aldith, and she was healthy and our fortunes were good. Ten years passed and I almost forgot what happened with the witch.

I got home late in the night and found the house covered with blood. Nolwen and Aldith were nowhere to be found. I ran outside looking for them and I found Nolwen there. She was dead, her throat ripped out. I searched the rest of the night for Aldith but couldn't find her. The next morning she was back in her bed as if nothing happened. I asked her but she said she didn't remember anything about the night. The next day I buried Nolwen and moved to another house closer to town where I thought we would be safer. I bolted the doors shut and thought we were safe. That night the moon was full, and I heard noises up where Aldith was sleeping. I ran up there and she was changing. I saw it with my own eyes. She changed into a wolf! The wolf attacked me and I was able to beat it back with a club. It jumped out through the window and disappeared.

Late in the night, she returned, human again but covered with blood, especially around her mouth. I knew it wasn't her blood. I went to town and heard about the wolf attack. Tye and his wife were killed that night by a wolf, in their own house!"

"I chained up Aldith that night, not knowing what else to do, but the moon was waning and she didn't change. The next night I thought it safe to keep her out of the chains, but in the middle of the night she tried to stick me with a knife. She is devious and will make you think she is innocent, but even when the moon is not full she is dangerous. But she is not evil. It is the spell."

Alec returned to Aldith's house and found it empty. He was too frightened to go back to the smithy, and knew she wouldn't be there, so he decided to go to the village green where he knew there would be many people.

To his surprise, it was almost deserted. He saw a few men by the great tree holding spears around something on the ground. He approached and saw the wolf so trapped by the roots that it could not move a muscle, its eyes yellow with fear. It whined pitifully when it saw Alec.

"What's happened?"

"This beast attacked your sister Alec. Your mother saved her just in time and did this with magic."

Alec burned with hatred for the wolf. "Why didn't she kill it!"

"She was about to but Cedric the blacksmith came shouting that she was his daughter! Did you know he had a daughter Duncan?"

"No, he must have kept her hidden."

"I heard rumors he had one but we thought it was malborn and couldn't leave the bed-"

Alec staggered off as the men continued to talk. He vomited and sat down on the edge of the village green, feeling weak. In one moment he found out his mother was an elf, his love was a wolf, and he was a criminal for setting her free. He was relieved beyond words that Cedric was still alive, but although there was no chance that he was seen by Cedric, he was still terrified that his crime would be discovered. He looked over at the wolf in the distance and wished his father were here to tell him what to do. Crawling into a little cave formed by the hedges, he just sat there and waited.

...the ballroom as it was in its original glory

Terrell's Fifth Night - The Ball, Troll Attack

On the fifth night Terrell woke up to the sound of a bell tower striking midnight. He could hear voices coming from outside his room. He dressed and belted his sword and opened his door. He was amazed at what he saw. Instead of the crumbling, decrepit hallway, it was gaily painted and clean. Lamps shone brightly on their sconces every ten feet along the wall. Merry voices could be heard from down the hallway.

Cautiously, his sword raised, he walked down the grand hallway and saw there below the ballroom as it was in its original glory. A ball was in progress. A hundred or more couples dressed in the finest ball gowns and suits whirled gaily along the dance floor. An orchestra was set up on the dais and played the most exquisite melodies. A thousand candles lit the hall as brightly as midday. Along one wall were long tables spread with sumptuous food and drink of every variety.

Entranced, he sheathed his sword and slowly came down the stairway. He passed by a guard dressed in a fine, spotless uniform. Terrell noticed his sword was for parade, not a fighting sword. The guard paid him no heed.

At this part of the dance everyone held hands and formed a great chain and circumnavigated the hall. The dancers whirled by him so gaily that he could not keep from smiling. A woman in a bright blue dress grabbed his hand and suddenly he was in the chain dancing with them. She was young and beautiful and smiled at him like someone she had known and loved for years.

The dancing continued and he felt enchanted and could not look away from her eyes, only unlike the other night he sensed that she and all of these people were not malevolent. Whether he danced for minutes or hours he couldn't be sure. But the spell was suddenly broken.

Her eyes shifted to see something behind him and her

smile turned to horror. He turned to look and saw the glass doors at the end of the ballroom explode inward. Men and women screamed in terror. Seven hideous trolls, at least twelve feet tall, stormed into the ballroom. They each wielded a club and began cutting down the dancers like wheat.

Terrell drew his sword and the blade began to glow with an eerie blue light. He attacked the nearest troll, fighting as gracefully as he had danced only moments ago. The troll seemed surprised at being attacked and a blow to its leg quickly brought it down, then he finished it with a strike through the heart.

The guards were putting up a valiant defense but their show swords were powerless against these supernatural creatures' armored skin. Terrell continued fighting and his magic sword cleaved through the trolls like ripe fruit. The other humans had by now either fled or were killed. He lost track of his dancing partner amidst the fighting.

Finally he came to the last, and biggest troll. He managed to bring the creature down by ducking under its club blow and cutting open its heel. With a final thrust he killed the creature but in its death throes it struck him in the head. He swooned and fell unconscious.

Alec saw the first red rays of the sun appear. During the night the guards had changed, but other than that nothing was different. The wolf had not moved or uttered a sound, not even a whine. One of the guards gasped and he pointed down at his prisoner.

In front of his eyes, the wolf transformed into Aldith in a matter of seconds.

The guards shouted and one ran off.

Alec was still too afraid to move so he just watched.

The guard quickly returned with a blanket and a saw. The

men sawed Aldith free, wrapped her in a blanket and carried her to the bell tower, where Alec knew there were cells.

Confessions

In the cottage was Wyn, Julia, who returned late in the night, and Nessa, who now was upstairs in bed sleeping comfortably. Her wounds had been cleaned and dressed and given a sleeping drought which put her to sleep. Luckily the wolf had not had time to do more than wound, although her leg was so badly damaged Wyn was fearful she would never walk again.

She heard someone enter the cottage and she climbed down the ladder.

Alec stared at his mother, whatever spell that made her appear like a human woman was gone. She looked wild and powerful. It frightened him, yet he was proud. His mother was an elf and even though he suspected this for some time, he was still surprised.

Wyn had already heard of the full confession by Cedric, and could guess from her son's behavior about his involvement.

"Tell me what you did last night."

Alec told her the truth but broke down when he said he thought he killed the blacksmith.

"The beast you set free almost killed your sister," she said coldly.

"I know. But I still love her."

"Go to her then!"

Bunwych had no proper jail but the bell tower had cellars with stout doors which served in times of need. Alec returned there. Many kegs of wine and beer were hastily scattered about and several men were around taking barrels away. No one noticed when he entered, descending the stairs to the cells. He passed one door with a barred window. Alec peeked inside and saw false Liam wrapped in a blanket, cowering in the corner of the cell.

Confused, he went to the next door and looked inside. Aldith was there wrapped in a blanket on a cot, facing the other way.

"Aldith."

She made no response.

"Aldith, it is Alec."

"Go away Alec. I am a monster."

"I know there is some kind of curse on you that makes you change like that."

She stirred, sat up and turned to him. Her eyes were red from crying.

"How did it happen? There must be some way to break the curse."

She told him the entire story as Cedric told it, although she cast herself as victim and didn't mention the people she attacked.

"I will find some way to break the curse."

"How?"

"I will find and destroy the witch."

Midsummer's Day

The next morning Terrell woke groggily. Blood was crusted over his eyes. He blinked to clear them and rose. He was in the ballroom, but it was again ruined just like the day he first came to the castle. But it was not exactly like it was. The feeling of dread seemed to be gone. A thought suddenly struck him. He ran up the stairwell to the third floor hallway. Quickly he found what he sought, a painting of a young woman, the same woman he danced with the night before. He gazed into her eyes and knew he was in love. In despair, he realized the woman he was in love with had been dead for over a hundred years. He took out a bottle of wine and spent the day drinking it.

Julia took out the mirror which she had hidden under her bed, and snuck off to the barn. She climbed the wooden ladder up to the hay loft and arranged an area to sit. She held up the mirror and viewed herself with displeasure. Her hair was tangled and she hated her ears which she judged as entirely too big. She fixed her hair then said, "Faerie Queen?"

The lens of the mirror became clouded as if from smoke and after a few seconds it cleared and there in the mirror was the face of the faerie queen.

Julia was sitting but bowed her head and said, "Your Majesty."

"Julia my child, it is good to see you."

"Something terrible has happened last night during the solstice festival. Nessa was attacked by a wolf but mother used her magic to save her just in time."

"Nessa survived?"

"Oh, yes, but mother said she may not walk again."

"My magic can heal her. Your mother is a fool."

"Oh, and also a boy attacked a little girl. He almost drowned her but she was saved by another boy who looked just like him! He knows magic! They are like twins, only one is wicked and the other good."

"How terrible. Where are these boys now?"

"Oh the good one is back with his family and the wicked one is locked up I expect."

"It was lovely to speak to you, my child, but I must go now. I will see you again soon."

With that, the mirror became cloudy again then once more like an ordinary mirror.

Confessions – The Curse

Glancing up at the spoons hanging from the wall, Wyn saw that Nessa's spoon had mostly regained its shine, but Morris' was now darkening. She rushed up to him. He was asleep but having a terrible nightmare. Wyn shook him awake. His eyes opened, bloodshot and watery. She knew how the dying looked, and knew he wouldn't last another day.

"Oh my boy, what is wrong with you?" she whispered as she cradled his head.

Morris looked over and saw Nessa sleeping in the next bed, covered with bandages.

"What happened to Nessa?"

"She was attacked by a wolf."

"Mother, I have to tell you something. I was playing with Nessa in the Dark Forest when she was just gone. I looked for her and found her in a hut with a witch. She was going to put her in the oven. I pushed her in the oven instead and we ran away. A few days later an old lady I have never seen was in the woods carrying firewood. She needed help so I took the firewood. All of a sudden she changed into the witch and said I had taken the curse. I'm sorry Mother. I should have told you."

"Where did this happen?"

"On the path to town."

"Where exactly? It is important Morris."

"The path to the river, where it crosses the road."

"A game of cards. If you win you may take my soul. If I win, you remove the curse from my child."

Wyn's Revenge

The witch was in her pig pen, ankle deep in the mud and waste, but not minding. She was stroking and muttering nonsense to her smallest piglet when she suddenly cocked her head, sensing Wyn's presence. Although they had never met, the witch knew of the faerie queen's daughter and her great power. Peering through the twisted fence branches, for a moment terror was in her eyes. This quickly passed, however, as she remembered that here, in her domain, none was more powerful. Wyn walked calmly and confidently into the small clearing surrounding the hut. Rage was not in her eyes. Instead there was perhaps even a trace of a smile.

The witch kicked at a pig in her way, which squealed and ran off, swung open the pen door, which was made of twigs wound together, and shambled over to meet the elf.

"I will not take back the curse, couldn't even if I wanted," the witch said, looking down at the ground.

"I come to offer you a bargain, Witch of the Dark Wood."

"A bargain, you say? Tell me!" The witch loved bargains. They always turned out in her favor, for she would always cheat.

"A game of cards. If you win you may take my soul. If I win, you remove the curse from my child."

"Trumps?" the witch said eagerly.

"If you wish."

"I deal! No magic!"

"Very well," Wyn said, then waved her hand casually in front of her. Immediately three stones rose up out of the ground, two seats, and a small table. The witch tried to look unimpressed with the display of magic, which should not have been possible so close to her home and source of power, and both sat down.

Wyn took out a deck of cards and placed them on the table

in front of the witch.

She eagerly took the deck and began to shuffle. Her ancient hands, like the gnarled wood which penned in her pigs, dealt painfully slowly, muttering numbers to herself with each card. Gradually, three piles of three were dealt to each player, with the top card face up. The remaining cards dealt evenly to both players.

Finally, all the cards were down and the players examined their decks. Wyn played the first card, a seven of cups, placing it on one of the witch's piles, and drew another from the deck. The witch played a nine of cups, and drew another, visibly pleased with the result. Wyn next played a king of cups, and the witch followed with a trump card, the chariot.

"Prize?" the witch asked.

Wyn waved her hand, signaling her to take the pile.

The witch cackled and slid the cards closer possessively.

The game proceeded with the witch starting the next trick. She placed a three of swords on one of Wyn's piles, concern on her face. Wyn followed with a five, and the witch with a jack. Wyn then played a trump, the hermit, and the witch played a higher value trump, the hanged man. The witch licked her withered lips and eagerly grabbed at the cards. Wyn held out her hand and the witch froze, then played a higher ranked trump, justice. The witch jerked her hand away and looked into the faerie's eyes, which now showed unfettered hatred and disgust.

"No magic!" the witch objected.

"No magic," Wyn reassured, icily calm once again.

The game continued and the witch took the next pile, and Wyn the following.

The next trick began and many cards were played. Whoever won this trick would doubtless win on points. Wyn played a jack of pentacles and the witch followed with the fool;

the highest ranking trump, Wyn had lost.

"My trick! I win!" the witch cackled as she greedily slid the cards over. She looked up, expecting to see a defeated, dejected opponent. Instead, Wyn was laughing, raw hatred flashing in her eyes.

"No fool! I win!" she said, standing up.

The witch stared at her for a moment uncomprehending, then panic and despair came over her like a cold gale. Her clawed hands desperately turned over the cards one by one, hidden under one was the small parchment with the runes she herself had scrawled.

"No! You cheated! Not fair! Shame on you!" the witch shrieked. She got up and staggered toward the false safety of her hut, tripping once, finally reaching her door and vanishing inside.

"Your hut will not shelter you. The curse is strong. You made sure of that," she said softly to herself.

Wyn stood there motionless, watching the hut, keeping vigil for hours until sunset came.

Alec followed the path to the witch's hut. He saw his mother standing there, her dark hair down and blowing wildly in the breeze. She seemed like a stranger.

"Alec, you should not be here."

"She knows how to cure Aldith!" he shouted.

"Speak not her name to me. That beast almost killed your sister." She turned back toward the hut. Her eyes became glassy. "The witch is near death."

Alec glared at his mother then marched into the hut. The witch was lying on her cot, motionless. Her eyes were closed. Her spider familiar was there on her chest, keeping vigil.

Alec stared at the hag in disgust. Before he could speak the witch said, "That which you seek is not here. Now go, leave me to die."

"Tell me how to break the curse or I will destroy your spider," Alec said in the strongest voice he could muster.

The witch opened her eyes and slowly turned towards Alec. "A glowing crystal holds your love's soul. I will tell you where it is, for if you go to seek it you will be slain and that would please me. Go find the Great Wyrm of Orobas. She guards it."

Alec was satisfied this was the truth and turned to leave. As he did so she said, "She will burn you," and began cackling.

Without looking at his mother, Alec marched past.

"You will go back to the village and will not leave our home until I return," she commanded.

Alec did not look at her or respond.

Wyn patiently waited and more time passed.

The sun was setting. Wyn could sense the witch was near death, but even that was not enough to satisfy her thirst for revenge. She took three long strides to the door of the gnarled hut, held out her palm and the dry, fuzzy vines and twigs near her hand ignited, spreading within seconds to the roof and other walls. Stepping back from the intense heat without taking her eyes from the fire, she continued to watch until all was left was the rough stone chimney and the witch's oven, the same oven which nearly baked her own child. All that remained now was to spread salt among the ashes to purify this part of the forest, but that could wait until daylight.

Terrell's Sixth Night - Funeral

On this night Terrell had no fear of supernatural enemies. With the help of the wine he managed to fall asleep. At midnight he awoke and sat up. A slim figure stood silhouetted in the doorway.

"Come in," he said.

She took a step forward into the light. It was she, his girl.

"You are alive!" he exclaimed.

"No my love, I am only here in spirit. I was determined to thank you for your bravery," she said.

He reached out to touch her but could not. She was incorporeal.

"But I was with you last night. You were real," he said.

"It was powerful magic and your own dauntlessness that made last night possible. And because of your courage our spirits are now free of this prison." She smiled but there was also a measure of sadness in her voice.

"If magic brought me to you last night then I will find magic to return to you," he said determinedly.

"No my love, that is not possible. I must join my family and our people in the other-world. Do not be sad, perhaps we will meet again some day. Now I must go-"

She was fading out even as she spoke the last words. He reached out to her but she was gone. Sensing something, he rushed to the window.

Outside was a silent procession of spectral wayfarers. At the front, mounted on a pale horse was the aged king, his long, white hair flowed past his crown down to his shoulders. Next was the queen. She wore a long gown of royal blue, although the true color of the garment seemed muted and drained in the pale moonlight. After the queen was her, his lady. He lamented not even knowing her name. He considered calling out to her, but dared not disturb the solemn parade. Behind her was doubtless her younger brother aged perhaps fourteen. His hair, blonde like his sister, was cropped short like a helmet. He wore a crisp, blue uniform and shining black boots. Past the royal family were some dozen or so courtiers also grandly dressed in parade finery. Finally in two columns at the back were a hundred soldiers in light armor, armed with their flimsy parade swords.

He watched until the column passed out of sight. For a moment he considered following, but his instinct of self preservation checked this, as he knew the living would not be allowed to join the dead.

He wept in despair all night.

Two Days After Midsummer's Eve

The Second Wedding

The following morning Terrell resolved to put the matter of the girl behind him and return to the king, his mission accomplished. Gathering his belongings, he made to leave, hesitated, then turned to look at the girl's painting one last time. "I don't even know her name," he said aloud.

He passed by the castle walls and into the orchards leading to town. He passed into the town and saw a commotion from the village green. A large group of people were gathered. Getting closer, he could see that they were dressed in their finest clothing and garlands of flowers were displayed in multitudes.

Alcot ran up to him, "Morning Sir Terrell!" he said cheerfully.

"Morning lad. Is this a wedding?" he asked.

"Yes, Lyneth is marrying the King of the Dwarfs," he said.

Before he could process this, Galvin approached and said, "Good morning Sir Terrell. I see you are carrying travel bags. Is your business here finished?"

"Yes, I'm afraid so. You have my word I will do my best to ensure this town is not harmed."

Galvin smiled sadly and said, "Thank you Sir Terrell, but I fear the fate of the town may be out of your or my powers."

Terrell considered telling him of his true rank in the court, but then for the first time saw the bride, who was dressed all in white. It was she! The girl he danced with. His love. The same golden hair, the same blue eyes. She was upset, crying. He searched the crowd for the groom. There was the mad dwarf he saw in the giant's lair. He wore a crown like a king. Another dwarf was speaking.

Argrim said aloud, reading from a scroll, "..and following completion of all three heroic tasks; separating a bushel of oats and a bushel of barley, slaying the giant Galifron in single combat, and felling a stout tree with nothing but water-"

"He did not slay the giant!" Terrell shouted.

Every man, woman, and child turned to stare at the knight, mouths agape.

King Gomrund turned beet red.

Arngrim shouted back, "This man lies. Our valiant king defeated the giant and brought back his finger as proof!"

Terrell boldly took a few steps forward. "That is false! I poisoned the giant. When I was leaving his lair I saw this one groveling at my feet, begging me for mercy!"

Arngrim was about to continue the debate when he saw out of the corner of his eye, his king run across the lawn and disappear through a hedgerow. He turned to follow him, running with as much dignity as possible.

The crowd gave out a great cheer. Tomos, the bride's father, was jubilant and said to him, "We are forever in your debt!"

Terrell accepted the wine offered to him but carefully watched the bride. She was clearly happy that the wedding was off. She looked at him. *Does she recognize me?* he wondered. *Could she really be her?*

He pushed through the crowd that was lauding him and walked up to Lyneth.

She smiled and said, "Thank you for making that horrid little man run away."

"It was my pleasure," he said. She didn't know him. Could

she be the same, or was it his imagination?

He took her arm and led her on a walk around town. They talked much, of nothing in particular. Her voice seemed the same, but he could not be sure. If only there were a way to find out for certain. Then he remembered the painting in the castle.

They returned to the village green. The crowd had dispersed but Lyneth's father and mother were still there. He bade her goodbye, politely kissing her hand. Tomos looked pleased.

Terrell Helps Galvin

Terrell returned to the castle and ran up the stairs to the painting, took it down and studied it carefully in the light. There was a small birthmark clearly painted on her left cheek. He searched his memory but could not recall a matching mark on the village girl. It was too late to see her again so he would have to wait until morning. He now faced a dilemma; to do his duty and return home, and possibly seal the destruction of Bunwych, or break his sacred vow to his king and father, stay in town and marry a commoner. He paced the castle grounds in deep distress. Finally, he resolved to see Galvin and find out anything he could about the castle and its inhabitants.

Terrell found the house of Galvin and knocked with the brass knocker mounted on the door. There was a commotion inside, many small voices chattering and numerous small feet pattering. He knocked again. Finally the door opened a crack. A tiny goblin, just a foot tall, stuck his enormous nose out and said coarsely, "What do you want?"

"I wish to see Galvin, is he in?"

The door abruptly banged shut again. There was another chattering of voices sounding like an argument. Terrell knocked again.

The door opened a crack once more, and another, different goblin's nose protruded out. "The master is not at home," he said.

Another goblin voice from inside added, "Go away!" The door slammed shut again.

Confused, Terrell turned to leave. He walked past the house and chanced to see the garden shed around the corner. Through the small window he could see Galvin for an instant who quickly ducked down as if he were hiding.

Angered at being played the fool, Terrell marched over to

the shed and entered without knocking.

Galvin was crouched down underneath the window. He looked at first surprised, then quickly embarrassed.

"Why do you hide from me, old man?" Terrell demanded.

"What? Oh no, I am not hiding from you." Galvin sat down as if defeated. "Forgive me, I will tell you everything," he said.

Galvin told Terrell the story of how the first goblin arrived at his beckoning, how more and more came, and finally how he came to be put out of the house and took up lodging in his shed.

Being bold of heart, and never having lived in a small hamlet, Terrell could not grasp why Galvin was so embarrassed about the situation. He did, however, understand how the old man could fear the magical creatures.

Smiling, Terrell said, "I believe I have a solution to your problem." He took Galvin by the arm and led him to the back door of his house.

Both he and Galvin were shocked by what they found inside. The kitchen was in a horrid state. Dirty dishes were piled up in the sink all the way to the ceiling. The floor was strewn with numerous empty wine bottles. Several were broken. A pile of goblins were laying atop the kitchen table, and several more on the hutch, asleep.

Dozank and his cousins

They passed into the parlor. The room swarmed with countless goblins; drinking, cavorting, coughing, sleeping, dancing, laughing, fighting, playing cards, eating, vomiting, crying, itching, choking, juggling, spitting, smoking, whistling, and wrestling. The plaster walls had numerous holes, some large enough for a goblin to fit through. In fact, one goblin was asleep fully inside one of the holes. Scrawled on the intact sections of the walls were erotic drawings and obscene poems. A portrait of Galvin's mother which hung above the fireplace was now askew and someone had drawn a beard and mustache on her. Littering the floor were dirty linens, corks, filthy socks, eggshells, broken crockery, shaving soap, and a cup filled with a dried green substance, empty walnut shells, apple cores, feces, a dead mouse, sack cloth, wood shavings, a dried paint brush, several decks of cards strewn about, an empty pickle jar, two dead frogs, goose feathers, rabbit droppings, the neighbor's welcome mat, cracker crumbs, a rotten cabbage, a set of beads, rusty nails, the leg bone of a goat or sheep, a pile of coal, several broken bricks, a live crow, many large buttons, a pile of hair, a broken window, a torn hat, dried flowers (possibly roses), a horse shoe, a broken rake, rope knotted into a noose, a block of salt, broken goblin tooth, a spool of unwound thread, roofing shingles, and countless other items which defied description.

"My home! What have you done to my home? Get out you filthy monsters! Get out!" Galvin cried.

All at once a dreadful silence filled the room and every goblin turned their heads to Galvin, mouths agape.

Dozank jumped up on a table and looked Galvin in the eye and said, "What did you call us, you ungrateful, nasty human?"

Galvin's new found courage immediately dissipated and he turned red and looked down.

Terrell stepped forward and said, "Why do you faeries inhabit a hovel like this?"

"What! This is the finest house in all of Bunwych!"

Dozank said proudly.

"Finest?! Do you know that one of the grandest castles in the land is but a mile away."

This caused some commotion in the crowd.

Dozank said, "Yes, well, the faerie queen wouldn't allow it. We cannot serve unless we are invited by the owner of the property."

Terrell puffed up, and in his most solemn tone said, "I, Prince Terrell, heir to the great King Alfred, lord of this land and all it contains, give you permission to serve in the castle."

The goblins uttered a great cheer and all at once rushed for the door, quickly grabbing their belongings as they left. In ten seconds the house was goblin free.

"Oh, how can I ever thank you?" Galvin said, grabbing Terrell's hand with both his hands and shaking them up and down.

"Now that you mention it, I wanted to ask you about the last family that inhabited the castle. Do you have any knowledge of them?"

"No, but in my library there is a book, if they haven't destroyed it."

Galvin led him through a door into the library. The room fared better than the parlor, but there were many books strewn about and ripped. Galvin let out a cry of despair.

"It should be over here," he said sadly, reaching for a shelf and pulling out a large, old volume. "This contains a history of Bunwych." He opened it and began to read and turn pages for what seemed an eternity to Terrell.

"Ah, yes. Well, there is not much information. What do you wish to know?"

"The name of the king, his queen, his son and daughter."

"King Baglan and Queen Cordelia. Their son was prince Eirwyn and their daughter Princess Rowena."

Terrell let out an audible sigh.

Galvin looked up at him through his spectacles curiously.

"Thank you," he said and left the house as if in a daze.

It was suppertime and the four children of Wyn sat at the dinner table together for the first time in many days. By this time Morris was almost completely recovered and Nessa was well enough to get out of bed for short periods. Wyn had not spoken to the children about what happened the night Nessa was attacked. They were all finished and looked up at their strange new mother with a hushed awe and perhaps a trace of fear.

Wyn smiled at them and began, "Children, the time has come for me to tell you the truth. As you now know, I am not a human, but a faerie. An elf to be specific."

Nessa grinned and clapped her hands.

Alec burst out, "I knew it!"

Morris' eyes widened.

Julia showed no emotion.

"Hush. Twenty years ago, before Alec was born, I was living in the faerie queen's castle in Elfhame, the only daughter of the faerie queen.

"Every seven years on Samhain night the faerie queen must pay a tithe to Cernunnos, the horned god of the forest. This takes the form of a sacrifice. The sacrifice cannot be a goblin or pixie, it must be not just a faerie, but a high elf. The queen discovered that a human will satisfy Cernunnos, but only if he has been living with and amongst us for a time. So for many years the queen has lured humans to Elfhame, letting them eat our food and live amongst us.

"One day a man named Brogan was taken, your father. He was strong and wise and beautiful, and more honorable than any elf in court. We fell in love, but it was forbidden. The queen was proud and vain and would never let her daughter marry a lowly human. The time of the sacrifice was coming and we despaired of what to do. We were married in secret and fled across the river to Bunwych. When the queen found out she fell into a rage. She summoned an ettin, a ferocious giant with one eye, to kill us. It attacked during the night and nearly killed us, but together we managed to fight it off. Brogan wounded it in the eye, blinding it, and it ran off. I only found out last night that Cedric found it and finished it off, and that it was the offspring of the Witch of the Dark Forest.

"I was now pregnant with Alec and we settled down into this cottage. I cast many warding spells to protect us from the queen, who was angered still. I gave up my fine clothes and big palace and we lived like simple villagers but we were happy and together. I had Alec and Julia and Morris was on the way. One day Brogan was careless and crossed the river which kept us apart from Elfhame. The queen found him and cast a spell, turning him into a bear. He made his way back to me and I was able to dispel the curse, but only partially. By night he became a bear again. It was dangerous for him to be around you children so he set off to live by the mountain. The times he was human he was able to come back and be with us, but as the years passed, those times became more and more infrequent.

"The wild man I met...it was father!" Alec said.

"Yes, he thinks of you all much, even though he can't be here with us."

"I want to meet him," cried Morris.

"Yes, I do too," said Nessa.

"And you shall my darlings, but later, some day when it is safe."

Morris Meets His Father

After the curse was lifted and the witch died Morris slept deeply and peacefully. The next morning he awoke and felt as good as he ever had. He went to his tree house. The magic cap and the witch's broom were still there. After a moment's hesitation, he grabbed the broom. In a clearing near the river he prepared a fire. When it was good and blazing, he threw the broom on the fire. Instantly it burst into flame, and in only a minute was nothing but ashes.

Pleased at destroying the last remnant of the witch, he wandered off down to the river, finding himself drawn to the stream where the wild man, his father, lived.

Somehow he knew where to find him, by the cave just past the stream. He was sitting there in front of an extinguished campfire, looking at him and smiling slightly. Morris felt a little nervous but approached anyway. Brogan said nothing but kept on his pleasant smile.

"I am Morris, your son."

"I know," he said gently, laughter twinkling in his eyes. "Sit."

They sat there for a time, saying nothing.

"What do you do Morris?"

"I don't know. I swim, fish, play in the river."

"Come," Brogan said.

Brogan led him to a part of the stream that was wide and shallow, only a few inches deep. Many stones were in the bed of the stream and along the banks.

"The stream here is choked. The fish cannot pass to spawn. Move the rocks here to the sides so the water can flow and the fish can pass."

Now, like many boys of ten, Morris was lazy when there was real work to be done but he also wanted to please his father, and so began the work. Brogan left, heading back to camp.

After an hour Morris returned to the camp. "I am finished," he said, quite pleased with himself.

Back at the stream Brogan took a quick look at the work and said, "You have not finished. Here needs to be this deep, all the way to here," he said, motioning with his hands.

"But that will take days! Who cares about the stupid fish anyway?"

Brogan frowned and said gently, "Do not return until you have finished."

Morris worked the rest of the day until sunset, only completing a small portion of the work. He returned home tired and sore, his hands raw from the toil.

For the next three days, Morris worked non-stop, pausing only for sleep and meals. The task became a foe he had to vanquish. As he toiled he developed pride in his work, and felt a certain warm glow of satisfaction when he put his head down to sleep.

Finally, he was finished and he returned to his father's camp.

Brogan saw the stream and beamed with pride. Morris felt wonderful. They returned to camp and Brogan took out a water skin and handed it to Morris. It was new wine, sweet and with just a little kick of alcohol. They sat up for a while, watching the stars.

All of a sudden Brogan's eyes became glazed. Morris felt a prickling down his back. A strange expression took over his father's face, a grimace, as if he were in pain.

"You must go now," Brogan gasped.

Morris was frightened and could not move.

"Go!" he shouted.

Morris stood up and backed away.

"Run!"

Morris turned and ran all the way home.

Three Days After Midsummer's Day

Terrell didn't trust the goblins but they were good workers. They had already fixed the roof and were busy restoring the castle's living quarters. With this in process, Terrell packed a travel bag and a shovel and set off through town and back into the forest. He was heading back to the lair of Galifron, intending to bury his dead comrades.

After traveling most of the day he made it back to the cave. Inside the corpses that remained stank terribly but he wrapped a scarf around his face and completed the grisly work, burying them in a little meadow on the mountain.

With the lamp he brought he was able to get a better look at the giant's treasure pile. He found some more silver coins and a pretty silver trinket which he stuffed into his boot as he started off back to the castle.

Julia was speaking to the faerie queen with the mirror, as she did every day since the night of the solstice.

"Julia my love, I have missed so many of your birthdays. What can I give you? Jewelry? A new dress? A love charm perhaps?"

She hesitated, turning beet red.

"Of course. Who is it you wish to use it on?"

She hesitated, embarrassed, then finally said, "There is a knight who came recently to the town. His name is Terrell."

"Julia. It saddens me that you waste your heart on a mere human."

"Oh no, he is no mere human. He is a knight, and very strong and brave. They say he killed the giant Galifron."

"I see I must educate you since your mother will not. I will devise a test for this gallant knight so you can see what humans are really like. Come to the faerie bridge at noon."

Julia did as she was bid and went to the faerie bridge. She was there only a moment when a white shape emerged from the faerie side of the bridge. She gasped. It was a unicorn; a perfectly formed milk white pony, with blue eyes and a single long narrow horn. It approached her shyly, then knelt down before her. She felt compelled to mount it. As soon as she did, the unicorn trotted off, heading away from the village. It's gait was so smooth the Julia rode it effortlessly despite not having a saddle.

The unicorn took Julia to the faerie palace where the queen greeted her and brought her to a room with a silver vessel filled with water. The queen waved her hand over the water and an image formed on the surface of the water. Julia could see a pretty meadow with wildflowers of great variety.

"Watch. I will return soon."

Fifteen goblins were toiling away at the castle, busy making the living quarters more habitable. Terrell was there supervising, marveling at how hard the goblins worked. He chanced to look out the window and saw there in the courtyard below the most magnificent white stallion as he had ever seen. It was riderless, but was dressed with a golden saddle and yellow reins of silk.

Quickly he ran down the stairway and emerged outside. The horse was calmly chewing some grass. Slowly and gently, he approached the horse, uttering soft noises.

He felt compelled to mount the horse. The horse allowed him to mount. But when he grabbed the reins, the horse suddenly took off at full speed. Terrell tried to rein in the mount but it did not heed his commands. In a heartbeat the horse and rider were traveling so fast the land flew by in a blur. Time became meaningless and after a period which could have been seconds, minutes, or hours, the horse began to gradually slow then stopped in a fine green meadow. The terrain was different. A majestic mountain rose up far higher than any he had ever seen. Terrell knew he was in a land far from Bunwych. The horse stood in the meadow calmly, as if waiting for someone.

Then, a lady appeared, emerging from a footpath leading into the forest. She wore a flowing green gown, golden shoes, and a bodice of yellow. Her long, graceful neck supported a beautiful and noble head with long, white hair, and was capped by a delicate golden crown. Although her hair was white she looked young, but something in her eyes made Terrell think she was actually very old.

"Who gave you leave to enter my land?" she said impassively, but with authority.

"I beg your pardon, Your Majesty, but this horse seemed to have a plan in mind before I mounted and he would not be dissuaded."

"Nevertheless, it is my meadow which you are standing on and I demand restitution."

"Restitution? Surely no harm has been done."

"The trampled wildflowers would feel otherwise. In fact, let us hear from them."

The faerie queen waved her hand over the meadow and what sounded like a hundred voices crying in pain and anguish assailed Terrell's ears.

"Again I beg your forgiveness."

"I have already forgiven you, but the butterworts and cornflowers are not so generous. In fact the primrose are most vindictive. I greatly fear that finding your way home will be more difficult than your journey here."

"Please my queen, ask them what I must do to make amends."

There was a pause when the queen seemed to be listening, then she said, "You must cross a bridge and enter a tall tower, defeat three foes, and solve three riddles. Only then will you be allowed to return home. Follow this path."

The faerie queen turned and motioned for Terrell to follow. This he did and he found himself in such a thick forest that he could no longer see the sky. A multitude of insects, frogs, birds, and many other forest creatures hummed noisily. The trees were thicker than the largest rain barrel and their bark wore a centuries growth of moss. The queen stopped and threw him a short piece of green cloth with three knots tied on it. When he looked back up the queen was no longer there.

Terrell continued to follow the path for some time until finally emerging into a clearing which bordered a steep cliff. Beyond the cliff rose up a tall, stone tower. The walls were of a smooth, white stone which fit together so closely that no mortar was visible. A stone bridge, two horse lengths wide, and thirty long spanned the cliff, leading to a door in the tower. Standing guard at the door was a knight in full armor which was a dull silver color.

In a moment of panic, Terrell realized he had no weapon, but a moment later he was dismounted and holding a sword and in full armor.

The guard was slumped over but then seemed to notice Terrell and without delay, charged at him with his sword held high.

Julia gasped in fright and glanced back as she suddenly noticed the queen had returned.

Terrell ran forward and met the charge. The valley echoed with the sound of metal clashing as the swords struck.

Terrell ran forward and met the charge. The valley echoed with the sound of metal clashing as the swords struck. The guard struck again and again and Terrell parried each blow. With each blow he could feel his opponent's guard weaken. At last his foe failed to parry a blow and Terrell struck him on the shoulder. His armor held but was visibly dented. Terrell charged forward and renewed his attack with even more force. The guard was off balance for a moment and Terrell charged and pushed him backward and landed heavily on the ground with a metallic clang.

Terrell stood over the guard who was breathing heavily and not attempting to rise. He took off the man's helm revealing long, gray hair and the face of an old man.

"Go ahead, finish me off. You are victorious."

Terrell considered for a moment then lowered his sword.

"Slay me! It is your duty!"

Terrell took his horse's reins and walked him toward the door. The guard began shouting obscene threats, slanderous challenges, and abusive obliques, which Terrell ignored. He looked down at the chord the faerie queen had given him, one of the knots was untied, only two were left.

Julia watched the entire battle without blinking or even breathing. Finally when Terrell won she took in a breath.

"He defeated the first foe!" she said.

The faerie queen answered, "The first challenge has passed but it was not defeating the guard, that was easy. It was showing him mercy, for this guard had been on duty for a hundred years, and if he died, your knight would have to take his place and guard the tower in perpetuity."

Terrell left his mount and pushed the massive door. It opened with a rusty creak. Inside was a large chamber dimly lit by a dozen flickering candles. Near the door was a young maiden, chained by the leg to a post in the wall. At the other end, against the wall, was a suit of armor, standing motionless.

"Please sir, unchain me," the girl pleaded, speaking in an archaic accent.

Terrell sensed something was amiss. He scrutinized the girl. She had a loose, white dress on in a style he had never seen. Her face had a pleading look but there was something uncanny about her eyes. He heard a sound behind him, a clank of armor, and turned, quickly drawing his sword. It was just in time. The suit of armor which he could see by the void behind the face mask, was empty, but had quietly crept closer when he was looking at the girl and had its sword raised, ready to strike.

He parried the blow and danced back. The armor continued its attack and Terrell was on the defensive, blocking the heavy blows with great difficulty. His foe was slow but he was also, being still clad in the full plate armor. Forced back against the wall now, he realized a change in strategy was in order.

Blocking the sword with his shield, he wheeled around and got behind the attacker, managing a solid hit on its sword arm which should have severely injured a normal foe, but there was not even a drop of blood. From behind he heard the prisoner gasp. Now, with the advantage of being on the offensive, Terrell continued the attack, raining down blows on the armored creature and causing it to stagger back. Although several blows should have disabled the enemy, it remained standing and countered with an attack on the winded Terrell. Now on the defensive again, he was being forced back. He glanced a look at the prisoner from the corner of his eye and saw there was blood staining her white dress. Edging closer to her as he fought, he got a good look at her face and had an idea. Suddenly turning around, he kicked at the girl's knee, causing her to scream and slump back. The false knight suddenly went down as if struck by a blow, but quickly recovered and got back up.

Now certain, Terrell delivered a fatal blow to the female prisoner. The armor collapsed to the floor, lifeless. Gasping for breath, Terrell sheathed his sword and looked down at the chord, one knot was left.

"He is clever too, I see, and observant," said the queen. Julia smiled proudly, but the faerie queen smiled back confidently, which made Julia nervous.

Terrell found a door at the far end of the room and climbed the stairwell leading up to another door. This he opened and he emerged into a bedroom richly furnished with a bed, couches, a dresser, a mirror, and an armoire. There was a balcony overlooking the valley.

A girl ran into his arms.

"At last I have been rescued!"

Julia noted that the girl was very beautiful and her cheeks burned with jealousy.

"For an eternity I have been imprisoned here, awaiting a hero bold enough to rescue me. Come, see what you have won."

Terrell looked down at the valley below. There was a city of white marble, clean and beautiful.

"The city is yours to rule as king, and I shall be your queen."

Terrell paused politely, considering the offer. Some sense deep in his core told him that glamour was involved and the city was not real, at least not what it appeared to be.

"That is a tempting offer my lady, but I must confess I love another."

"What is her name?"

Julia flushed, her heart pounding now.

"Lyneth," said Terrell.

Julia gasped as if the wind was knocked out of her and began to weep.

The third knot loosened and the girl and the castle faded away. Terrell found himself back at the flowery glen where he started. His armor was gone but the fine white horse was there, calmly grazing. Terrell mounted him and said, "Take us home. Now, what should I name you? I know, Gwidion."

"Do not waste any tears on such as he, my child, after all, he is only a man."

The queen waved her hand over the water and the image faded.

"Why don't you stay here in Elfhame where you belong, after all there is nothing left for you back there now."

"My sister and brothers. I will miss them."

"Bring them too then. They belong here as much as you do."

"May I think about it?"

"Of course, take your time."

Julia returned home but was morose and silent. Wyn watched her but said nothing.

The supper was stew with rabbit, turnips, onions, carrots, and barley. Nobody spoke much, not even Nessa. Julia was still morose and sulking about Sir Terrell, although Wyn didn't know about that. She watched the children silently and began to worry that she was somehow losing them. After she revealed her faerie ancestry the children behaved differently toward her. Nessa seemed in awe, Morris looked at her as if she were a stranger, and Julia was particularly furious. Alec seemed the least changed. If anything he was warmer to her, although he was aloof and distracted by his new found love.

Wyn waited until dinner was finished then ordered the children up to their room, but told Julia to stay and help her wash up. When Julia banged the pot against the wash tub a little louder than necessary for the third time, Wyn exclaimed, "What is wrong with you? Why are you acting this way?"

Julia, her face beet red now, exclaimed, "How could you make us live out here like this, when we could have lived in a palace!"

"You do not know what she is like! How can I make you understand what I saved you from?"

"Saved us! You just wanted to be with him! You were just being selfish!"

"We were happy! I never let you starve."

"I am going to live there and there is nothing you can do to stop me!" She threw the pot down with a bang and ran upstairs.

Wyn sat down at the table and cried.

Liam's family threw a picnic banquet in celebration of his homecoming. It took place on the lawn by the blacksmiths, right next to the river. There was Millard, Bess, Elinor, Kyla, and Liam. A table was set up with a white tablecloth and food was set out.

Liam felt awkward around his real family, especially his father, who acted very strange around him, never looking him in the eye. His sisters were very sweet and kind and he quickly bonded with them.

Near the end of the day, Millard very nervously took his son aside and took him on a walk down the river.

"We are all very glad to have you back son."

"Thank you, I am happy to be back."

"There is something I must tell you."

Liam looked over at him and waited.

"Your abduction. It was my fault!" he exclaimed, face turning red as if he had just lifted and released a great weight.

Millard could tell Liam didn't understand, so he continued, "One day before you were born, I wandered too far into Elfhame. I came to a great tent in the woods and there was the faerie queen and many other fair folk. They offered me food, and like a fool, I accepted for I was famished. She made me-" He stopped then looked down at his feet.

"No, that is not true. She offered me a bargain, that I would have great fortune in exchange for my first born child. She told me you would be brought up in luxury and given many opportunities. I was a fool and accepted. Can you ever forgive me, son?"

Liam looked up and said, "Yes Father, I forgive you."

Millard grinned and put his arm around Liam. "It wasn't so bad, was it son?"

"No Father, I had a great friend there. She taught me many things."

It was 2 AM. Terrell was sound asleep in his newly renovated king's bedroom. Dozank and his 14 cousins were far off in a ruined section of the castle, drinking, cavorting, playing music. An owl fluttered into the big ruined chamber and settled on an oblique beam twenty feet high. Only Dozank noticed and he watched curiously. After a moment it fluttered down to him and landed on a pile of rubble closer to the ground.

"The queen commands," it said and the goblins became silent and watched the bird.

"We obey. What is her bidding?"

"Find a boy child called Liam and bring him to the queen."

"Where do we find him?"

"Follow," said the owl who fluttered through the exit into the night sky.

"Come on lads, the queen commands!" Dozank shouted.

Some goblins muttered complaints under their breath as they rose from comfortable positions. They put on their caps of invisibility and hurried after the owl.

"Fetch the pushcart," Dozank said to Zabark and Brut, who muttered a complaint under their breath but turned and rushed off, back into the castle. The cart was filled with rubble which they pushed over to unload. Up in his bedroom, Terrell stirred.

They wheeled the cart outside and joined the others.

Anyone watching the blush of goblins make their way through town would see only a driver-less cart rolling along following an owl high above, almost invisible against the cloudless night sky.

The owl began to circle and the goblins came to a two story wood framed house near the river. They circled the house and peeked into the windows. Seeing no one, the more spry of the goblins climbed up to the second floor windows and peeked in. One signaled to the group below and they began to scramble up the wall like a train of ants. The window was opened silently and an octet of goblins were in the room. It was a large bedroom with three beds. One contained a boy. They lurched toward the bed. Zabark stepped on Gzork's toe who squealed and smacked his cousin in the head. Dozank hissed for them to be quiet.

Liam awoke, and by virtue of living in Elfhame most of his life, had faerie sight, and could see the eight goblins coming for him. He grabbed a heavy candlestick and held it up threateningly.

"He can see us!" Dozank said.

"Get out of here or I'll bash you all!"

His sisters had now sat up and were looking at Liam with sleepy bleary eyes, thinking he was having a nightmare.

Dozank quickly pulled out a long, cruel looking knife and held it to Kyla's neck. "Don't make trouble boy, just come with us," he said.

Liam's brow furrowed in bitter helplessness as he slowly put down the candlestick. Four goblins rushed to him and with quick efficiency, hog tied him and gagged his mouth. Elinor and Kyla, still in the foggy veil of sleep, merely watched as he floated across the room and out of the window.

"Liam!" Elinor shouted as he floated through the window and down.

The goblins loaded Liam on to the pushcart and quickly made for the faerie bridge.

When Terrell heard the sound of the goblins unloading the cart he sensed something was wrong and he came down to investigate. He saw the cart roll out of the building as if of its own volition. He rushed up to his room to fetch his sword and put on his boots, then ran back down and outside and into the inner courtyard. Seeing nothing, he circled around the keep. He came back around and went out through the outer gate. Bending down, he could see some cart tracks in the mud leading toward the village. He followed but lost the tracks on the cobbled road. He continued to walk through town, watching and listening for anything out of the ordinary.

Soon he heard the sound of the wheels over gravel and ran in its direction. He saw it rolling toward the faerie bridge. It was traveling quickly though not as fast as he could run and just before the bridge he caught it. The goblins were still invisible but the cart and the child tied up in it were still visible.

He ran in front of the cart and shouted, "Stop! I know it is you, my so called servants. Go back to the castle at once. I command you!"

They all became visible as they pulled off their hats. "We are sorry but we serve a higher master than you."

"Who is that?"

They hesitated. Terrell held up his sword at Dozank. "Tell me!"

"Our queen! We are compelled to obey her."

"Go then, but I will not allow you to take this boy."

With some grumbling and cursing under their breath the goblins released the cart and walked in the direction of the bridge.

Terrell untied Liam and released the gag on his mouth.

As they walked home Liam told Terrell his story, that the fairies wanted him back to be used as a sacrifice to Cernunnos.

"Why don't you stay in the castle? You will be safe there. Your family can live there too, enough rooms have been restored."

Alec's Quest

Alec disobeyed his mother's command and headed straight for the cave of the wild man, his father. He was there in human form tending his fire.

"Father," he said.

Brogan continued his work and did not look at the boy.

"What is the Great Wyrm of Orobas?"

"It is a dragon, an ancient and powerful one."

"How can it be slain?"

"It would take a mighty hero. Dragons are the most powerful of beasts. They are the size of a mill house and can breathe fire."

Alec wasn't afraid. He was coming into his power, the power of youth.

Brent was the keeper of the bell tower, an inherited honor which had been in his family for countless generations. His duties were to maintain the building and bell, and to ring the bell at the appropriate times. For funerals, the bell was to be rung once every thirty seconds for a full hour. For weddings, the bell was rung continuously for a minute after the completion of the ceremony. During festivals the bell was rung whenever Brent saw fit. In an emergency, in case of attack, for instance, the bell was to be rung every 5 seconds with a mallet instead of the clapper. This had not happened in anyone's lifetime until two nights ago.

Alec came to the bell tower and knocked on the front door of the living quarters. Brent answered and fetched a large ring of keys. He let Alec into the cellar hallway, then led Alec down the stairs into a hallway. They passed the cell holding false Liam, then came to the second door and Brent opened it.

Alec entered and Brent locked the door behind him. "Yell

for me when you are finished," Brent said.

Aldith was laying on a simple cot and sat up. "Alec!"

Alec sat down next to her and embraced her. "My mother killed the witch! I found out how to lift your curse."

"Is that possible? How?"

"Don't worry about that. I promise you I will find a way."

Tomas was plowing his field, except instead of the ox pulling, he had a bit through his mouth and was pulling the plow himself. Behind him, constantly lashing him with a whip were his daughter and wife, who shouted obscenities and accused him of being lazy. Then, he looked up and saw a vast army of dwarfs in the field, trampling his crops. King Gomrund appeared wearing a white wedding dress and veil and demanded his gold dowry back. Tomas then found himself at the spot where he buried the gold, and he started digging with his hands, which were now cloven like a pig. He dug and dug, going far deeper than the gold was buried. Looking back, he could see the king getting increasingly angry and began throwing acorns at him. Suddenly, he fell through the dirt into a vast underground cavern. Before him, a gigantic animal with the body of a mole and the head of a female dwarf, had the gold chest in its mouth and glared at him, as if daring him to chase. He ran after the mole, running on four legs like a pig. Behind him is Gomrund, his wife, and daughter, all chasing him and yelling a constant stream of epithets. They come to a chasm, and the mole falls off and disappears. He comes to the edge and cannot stop and he falls, and falls, and continues to fall into the blackness.

Tomas awoke partially and scrambled off the bed, hitting the ground with a cry of terror and pain and thinking in his dream that he was crushed and dead. Katrin awakened and seeing what happened, rushed over to her husband to comfort him, telling him he was dreaming. After a few moments Tomas became completely awake, but the nightmare was still fresh and clear in his mind.

He quickly dressed and went immediately off to the tool shed to fetch the shovel. He found the spot where he buried the gold and hurriedly began digging it up.

He took the chest to the castle and found Sir Terrell outside at a table, scrutinizing a plan the goblins had drawn up.

"Sir Terrell," he said, out of breath.

"Mr. Tomos, what is wrong?" Terrell stood up, for a horrible moment thinking there was something wrong with Lyneth.

"I know we owe you more than we can ever repay, but I must beg you one more favor!" He dropped the heavy chest down on the table. "This gold wears heavy on my conscience. I cannot have it in my possession an hour longer. Will you take charge of it and return it to the dwarfs for me?"

Relieved, Terrell smiled, clapped the back of Tomos and said, "It is a small thing. Consider it done."

Tomos, a great weight lifted off his heart, thanked Terrell and walked happily home, once again poor but carefree.

Alec would not be dissuaded. He needed a hero, and as it happened he knew one, Sir Terrell, who slayed the Giant Galifron. He returned to the cottage and found his sister Julia cleaning out the barn. He began helping her. She stopped and stared at him.

"What do you want?" she asked suspiciously.

Giving up any attempt at pretense, he spoke plainly, "Will you bring me to see your friend, Sir Terrell?"

She suddenly felt dizzy. Last night she resolved to forget him, but doubt crept into her mind. What if he loved another? That could still change.

"Why do you wish to see him?" she asked, suspiciously.

"To ask him to slay the Great Wyrm of Orobos."

Julia exploded, "You will do no such thing!" brandishing the broom threateningly at him.

"Why not?"

"Why should he risk his life to help your wicked girlfriend?"

"She is not wicked! She is cursed, just like father!"

Julia said nothing but her face remained defiant.

"Very well. I will go see him myself," Alec said, turning to leave.

As he turned, Julia, now a fierce she-devil, pounced on his back, knocking him to the ground and pulling at his hair. They wrestled on the floor of the barn. Alec struggled to throw her off his back, but finally succeeded, and Julia lay on the barn floor gasping for breath and covered with dirt. As he ran off she did not attempt to follow.

Alec strode into the castle courtyard pensively. Terrell was there inspecting the outer wall the goblins had begun to repair, judging its defensive capability.

"Sir Terrell," Alec said, bowing before Terrell.

Terrell turned and said, "Please get up lad, that is not necessary."

"I am Alec, son of Wyn. My sister is Julia."

Terrell smiled, "Alec, I am pleased to meet you."

He was about to say more but was interrupted by Julia running into the courtyard. A dog Terrell had adopted began to bark at her. She was covered from head to toe in dirt, worse than when he first met her when she was cleaning the rugs.

"Do not heed him," she tried to say but was desperately

out of breath from running.

Alec frowned and began, "I wish to ask you a great favor."

Terrell was confused but smiled and said, "Go ahead, ask. If it is in my power I will help you."

"I need your help to slay the Great Wyrm of Orobos."

"Alec! You have no right!" Julia screamed and clenched her fists. Alec thought at first she would attack him again but this did not come to pass.

"I have heard of this beast but I did not know it was real," Terrell said, and seemed to consider a moment. "Why do you want this monster slain?"

"My true love, Aldith, is cursed by the Witch of the Dark Forest. The dragon guards a jewel which can set her free."

"I see," Terrell said. He turned to look through the castle gates in the direction of town, and seemed to consider. He didn't want to leave Lyneth. Truly, he was afraid. Finally, he sighed, and said, "I sympathize with your problem, but it is not my quest and I cannot help you."

Julia beamed triumphantly. Alec hung his head and mumbled something, then began to walk slowly off.

A thought occurred to Terrell, and he said, "Wait Alec, I have a notion. It is a long shot but it just might work."

Alec led Terrell, who carried the chest of gold, to the entrance of the ancient salt mine. It was partially boarded up but easy enough for them to pass through. Terrell paused to light a torch then led Alec into the tunnel. There was one main passageway which they followed. Neither of them knew exactly the way to the dwarfs' domain, but knew if they kept heading deeper into the earth, they would find the dwarfs.

Finally they reached a stout wooden door, wide but only about five feet high. Terrell knocked. In a few moments a rusty creaking could be heard and the door slowly opened. A dwarf guard stood there in a dimly lit passageway.

"What is your business?" the dwarf asked.

"We wish to see the king and return his gold," Terrell said.

The guard furrowed his brow, looked from Terrell to the chest of gold three times then turned and marched off without a word, leaving the door open. Terrell and Alec followed.

They passed by many marvels of dwarf workmanship which both humans found breathtaking. Stone reliefs on the walls, expertly carved and a delicate bridge spanning a deep chasm. Intricate mosaic floors and walls made of brilliantly colored tiles. A long colonnaded arcade with shops to each side. This opened up into a huge cathedral-like chamber with vaulted ceilings and a throne towards one end.

King Gomrund sat there on his salt throne. His eyes widened when he saw there in front of him the one who had humiliated him in front of the entire village.

"King Gomrund," Terrell dropped to one knee and lowered his gaze respectfully.

These courtly manners pleased the king but his gaze remained stony. "You may rise," he said, just barely managing to hide his rage.

"I have come to return to you your gold on behalf of the bride's father."

The king gasped in surprise.

"I also wish to beg your forgiveness for foiling your quest and killing the giant before you had arrived. It was yours to kill." This also pleased the king, but he remained stoic.

"There is one more thing. This boy," Terrell motioned to Alec, who bowed. "Has a quest which requires a great hero. He came to me but I confess, I have not the courage. I thought perhaps you may be interested."

There was a murmur of excitement from the dwarfs. This offer pleased the king. He had truly begun to think of himself as a great hero. The taking of the giant's finger after all took courage and it was not his fault that the giant was already slain. The quest for the ice wyrm was also led by himself and was gravely dangerous, His humiliation at the wedding was terrible to bear. His subjects remained polite but he could no longer see the adoration in their eyes. He lost the moniker, "Giant Slayer." Now was an opportunity for redemption, and to gain a new moniker, "Dragon Slayer."

The king rose up and said, "Make preparations! Assemble our seven greatest warriors. Our quest will begin tomorrow."

Even Arngrim, having seen how depressed the king had been, did not object to the great danger.

The court, in one voice, gave a great cheer.

Alec said, "If it pleases the king?"

Gomrund motioned to the boy to speak.

"May I accompany you?" he asked.

"Very well. And our greatest poet will also come to record our deeds."

This was not what Terrell planned but it was too late.

Full of excitement, Alec returned to see Aldith in the jail. Cedric was there, a bandage still on his head. To Alec's relief and surprise, Cedric smiled and embraced the boy.

Alec told them what had happened with the dwarfs.

"We leave tomorrow!" Alec said.

"You are going too?" Aldith said.

"Yes, of course."

"I will come too," Cedric said.

Aldith was truly frightened at the possibility of losing the two people she loved most.

"Don't worry, I will return with the gem," Alec said.

Wyn was adamant about not allowing Alec to go.

"I will stay in the back and let the dwarfs fight," he assured her. "Father has given his permission!"

This seemed to stun Wyn, she said, "We'll see about that."

Wyn came to Brogan's camp, and not seeing him there, called out to him. He came to her in bear form.

"You gave him permission to go with the dwarfs?"

"I made him promise to stay at the back and observe and not to fight."

"Even so…to take such a risk for a girl that almost killed our Nessa."

"He loves her. You would have done the same for me."

"He is my child. I am not ready to let him go!"

"You must, or he will languish. Remember, human children must grow up much faster than elves."

"I know." She started to cry. Brogan took a step closer, then stopped, placing his head on her shoulder.

"I wish you could hold me."

The Dragon Quest

Alec slept very little that night. At dawn, he came down to the kitchen and saw Wyn there. She had packed a bag for him with food for the voyage. He was about to leave when Morris came down, still in his sleeping garb.

"Take this, you may need it," he said, holding out his magical red cap. Alec thanked him and gave him a hug, which was unusual, but Morris pretended not to notice.

So he set off and came to the West Bridge where Cedric was already waiting, dressed in a makeshift metal breastplate and helm and carrying a sword. They waited there for a time, until the dwarfs came into view through the trees.

Dwarfs do not ride horses, but they had nine pack ponies in the group, along with King Gomrund, seven of his best warriors, and a bard named Dorund who was smaller than the others and seemed younger, his beard having no gray in it. The king was in the lead and barely nodded to Alec and Cedric who joined the procession in the rear with Dorund.

They followed the road all day, never even stopping to rest. Alec was frightfully tired, but marched on without complaint. Dorund began a kind of chant which most of the other dwarfs joined. The words were in olde Dwarvish, a language Alec had never heard. The story was about an ancient king who heroically led an army against an elf invasion and withstood the siege against long odds.

At dusk they made camp in a clearing along the forest. A fire was built and they ate heartily. Alec was almost too tired to eat but he knew he would need the energy for tomorrow's march. After dinner the dwarfs settled down to sleep but Dorund played soothing music deeply into the night. As Alec nestled into his bedroll it occurred to him that this was the farthest he had ever been from home. Notwithstanding his excitement, Alec fell asleep almost instantly, being exhausted, but woke soon after and listened to the music a while before falling back to sleep.

Just before dawn they ate a quick breakfast then hastily resumed the march.

They passed by some scrubby pastures with sheep grazing. Soon they passed by some clusters of huts and then found themselves in a small town. The townspeople stared at the ramshackle collection of men, boys, and dwarfs sullenly.

The king stopped and addressed the group, "we should take this opportunity to replenish our stocks. Dorund! Find someplace to buy grain for the horses. Uther, fill our bottles from that well."

The townspeople began to come out of the buildings and stare at the dwarfs. Alec felt uncomfortable, feeling like something bad was going to happen.

A few of the humans approached and one spoke, "What brings a party of dwarfs out of the mines?"

"We are on a quest, the details of which do not concern you."

"A quest you say?"

"Aye, to slay the dragon Galifron."

The crowd became suddenly silent. Long ago the people in the town had found a way to placate the dragon. Every day they would lead a sheep up to the bottom of the mountain, which the dragon would later come and eat. Since this tradition started, the dragon stopped attacking the town and only occasionally will kill a human that strayed too close to the mountain. This arrangement was costly but much safer than the alternative, and they were reluctant for this to change.

"Why does this displease you? Surely the dragon is a nuisance to you."

"Many have tried to slay the dragon. None have

succeeded. You will only anger the dragon and cause it to come here to unleash its wrath."

"I promise you we will defeat the monster and this land will be free of it. Now, will anyone here try to stop us?" The king put his hand on his ax handle. Every other dwarf did the same.

There was a tense silence as the king looked back and forth across the crowd. No one moved.

"Ride on!" the king ordered.

The road split and they headed west into a barren, hilly land. The road seemed to gradually dissipate until at some point it was clear they were no longer on a proper road.

"Look!" one of the dwarfs shouted and pointed forward.

By mid day Alec could see the mountain Orobas rising up far into the distance.

For three days they continued toward the mountain, which never seemed to get any closer. Never did they see any man or sign of man, nor did they see any other living creature, not even a distant bird.

Finally they reached the edge of a dense forest and the mountain disappeared behind the trees. They followed a path leading up and at times could see the mountain through the trees, now very close. The king gave the order to stop and the dwarfs prepared for battle, picking weapons and armor out of the saddlebags. With the exception of the king, the weapons were all battle axes, which the dwarfs commenced to sharpen meticulously.

Kilbar knelt before the king, head bowed and held out a sword. Gomrund pulled the sword from its scabbard and in unison the dwarfs murmured something reverently. The sword was called Wyrm Biter, and was magical.

The sound of something very large moving suddenly came from up the path. Everyone froze.

"Prepare for battle lads, the wyrm comes!" the king shouted. The dwarfs assembled quickly into formation.

Dorund ran and grabbed Alec, who was frozen and staring up ahead, and pulled him back with him. They ran far back into the trees, ducking behind a thick bush. Alec could see nothing through the branches, but was too afraid to move. He heard the dragon coming closer, unimaginably huge. The dwarfs shouted a war cry. There was the terrible sound of the dragon breathing fire like thunder followed by cries of pain. The ponies screamed and bolted off, one passing close by the bush, its coat smoldering. There was more shouting and the sound of metal striking metal, or was it metal striking dragon scales? More fire breathing thundered and more cries of pain and anger. Then, the sound of the dragon thudding away, followed by an eerie silence. The entire battle took only seconds.

Dorund carefully looked up over the bush, then poked at Alec, signaling him to follow.

Most of the area was blackened and smoking. There was the horrible smell of burning flesh and hair. Charred black forms in the shape of dwarfs lay on the ground smoldering. There was no movement. One of the shapes moaned. Alec and Dorund ran over to him.

It was the king. His eyes, the only thing not black with soot, opened. He reached out to Alec and pulled his shirt toward him. "My sword found a chink in its scales, it still is lodged, near its heart. It needs only a push and the glory will be yours. Go, finish this," he said, then died. Dorund began to sob.

Alec took out the magic cap and put it on. He looked back at Dorund but he was helpless, in the depths of grief. He followed the path upward and came to a bend. Rounding the bend he saw the yawning mouth of a great cave. Alec felt panic building inside. He closed his eyes and pictured in his mind the view from the top of the mountain during his fathers second lesson. A feeling of calm washed over him and he stepped into the dark cave.

The most striking thing about the dragon was its size. It was the size of the mill house in Bunwych. Its dinner plate sized scales were the color of rust mottled with black and gray spots. The dragon's head was narrow, with deep set black eyes separated by a bony ridge. It had four short, powerful limbs with three digits on each foot that ended in sharp claws. The dragon was obviously in distress, writhing on its back, the hilt of the sword sticking out of its chest. It was trying to reach the sword but it's forelegs were too short to reach.

Alec came closer, placing each foot carefully so as not to disturb a single pebble and make the slightest noise.

The Great Wyrm of Orobos

The dragon turned and looked directly at him. "Do you think I cannot see you there?" Its voice was intelligent and cold but not evil as Alec would have expected.

Alec was terrified, but quickly recovered and resolved to show no fear. He took off the cap and boldly glared at the dragon.

"Please, I entreat you, pull this cruel sword out and I will reward you richly," it said. Begging was in its voice.

"Why should I? You killed my friends!"

"They were coming to slay me. I was only defending myself. Do I not have that right?"

"You are evil, you kill innocent people, thousands."

"Do you think all tales are true? I am content to live here in my cave, hunting sheep or deer only when I need to eat. Is that evil?"

Alec considered. He was here to slay the dragon, but that was not his true goal, he only wanted to save Aldith. His mother would kill the dragon, he was certain. He tried to imagine what his father would do and remembered the lesson with the fly, and how he felt when he attacked Cedric and thought him dead. If he had nothing to gain by killing the dragon then it was wrong. His quest was to return the gem.

"Do you promise to not harm me and let me take something from here which I need?"

"This I gladly promise." The dragon crouched down in a submissive manner.

Alec took a step closer and grabbed the pommel of the sword. He hesitated, looking up at the dragon.

He pulled out the sword.

The dragon gave a great sigh of relief and rose up, unfolding its wings and showing its full scale. Alec cowered back, afraid again.

The dragon then swatted at Alec with its wing, sending him flying backwards and to the ground which caused the wind to be knocked out of him and the sword to clatter to the ground, several yards away.

"You are fortunate my fire is spent," the dragon hissed.

"You promised. Have you no honor?" Alec said, gasping for air.

The dragon reared up fiercely, "You puny human. You dare speak to The Great Wyrm of Orobos of honor? I have seen a thousand full moons. I have destroyed empires; melted the greatest castles to glass. A hundred kings I have slain and ten thousand champions. My spawn have spread to the furthest reaches of the land."

"Don't you care about anyone but yourself? What about your children?"

"This idea is alien to me. You milk drinkers fawn over your young, coddling them for years, pink and helpless. A newly hatched dragon can kill a horse."

"You say that like it is something to brag about."

"It is merely the nature of things. I have no need to brag. Tell me, what vexes your conscience? I smell it hanging over you like a dark cloud."

Alec looked down, "I caused my friend to die."

"Interesting! Tell me more."

"We were up on a cliff teasing the old ogre that lives down in the valley. I threw a rock. The ogre became enraged and attacked, almost reaching us. We ran away but Nolan slipped and fell off the cliff. The ogre ate him." Alec's voice quavered and tears welled in his eyes.

"I don't understand, why do you feel responsible for his death?"

"If I hadn't thrown the rock he would still be alive."

"Surely the blame is on the boy who got too close and was too clumsy to get out of the way without falling."

Exasperated, Alec said, "I guess you couldn't understand since you have no conscience."

"This thing you say I lack is a strength. What good does it me?"

"Maybe it doesn't do you any good, but if there are others around it can help you, like me pulling out the sword."

"But your conscience made you pull out the sword which was foolish, whereas I, who am free of this madness, benefited."

Alec said sullenly, "Well, maybe it is a weakness sometimes but you can't just turn it off. I guess you just have to be born with it."

"You amuse me. Perhaps I will let you live and be my slave. Wait here while I go back to eat your friends. " The dragon plodded off.

Alec was tempted to run away, escape, but he refused to give up. He ran to grab the sword, contemplating ambushing the dragon when it returned, but that was madness. He put the sword down, hiding it under some treasure. He began to search the enormous cave, trying to find the jewel. On the floor of the cavern were strewn countless coins and gems, hundreds of chests, tapestries, golden trinkets of every shape. He despaired. How could he find the gem he needed? He didn't even know what it looked like. He heard a noise. It was the dragon returning. He rushed back to where the sword was and sat down on a chest.

The dragon returned and nestled comfortably into a depression in the center of the cavern.

"You did not flee, why?" asked the dragon.

"I wont leave without the gem I was promised."

"Once an escaped slave stole a single cup from me when I was out hunting. I tracked him for a hundred leagues, burned down his village, and slayed every last one of his people. Do you think I would let you steal a treasure from me?"

"It is no treasure to you but it is precious to me."

"What riddle is this? What do you speak of?" said the dragon, intrigued.

"It is something that will heal someone I love."

"I believe I know of what you speak; the Crystal of Yalathanil. It is unique, a gem the size of an apple. I would never let it go. You were wise not to slay me, for you would have never found it."

"It is already gone. When you were off eating my friends I found it and threw it off of the cliff into the lake below to fetch later."

The dragon rose up in rage and turned, took five mighty steps into the depths of the cave toward an alcove. It stopped suddenly when it realized the trick, then more calmly, turned and moved back toward Alec, hovering over him malevolently. He could smell the acrid sulfur on the dragon's breath.

"You are clever but it will do you no good. Even if I let you leave here alive I would not let you take a single copper coin from my horde."

"Then you must die!"

Alec lunged forward with the magic sword, aiming for the gap between the scales on its chest, plunging the sword up to the hilt, and piercing the great dragon's cold reptilian heart. The dragon, in a last convulsion, swatted at Alec, launching him twenty feet across the cavern where he landed unconscious.

When he awoke, the back of his head was bruised but there were no other wounds. He returned to the bodies of his friends. He was horrified to find all of the bodies gone and

Dorund missing.

Alec heard a twig snap behind him. He turned and saw Dorund approaching from the trees. His face was streaked with tears.

"I killed it," Alec said solemnly.

Dorund grinned and embraced him.

They split up and searched for any of the surviving horses. Alec found one far into the woods in a grove of trees, its reins tangled in the branches, which stopped it from fleeing further.

They led the horse back to the cavern but it would not go inside. They left it there. Alec searched the alcove the dragon had moved toward when he tricked it into thinking he found the crystal. There were several chests. Inside the first two were nothing but coins. In the third were some silks and a small box. He opened it, inside was a gem the size of an egg. Through the white crystal he could see wispy shapes moving like smoke. It felt warm to the touch. Alec knew he found the stone.

He carefully packed the stone into the ponies' pack along with as much gold as it could comfortably carry.

When they reached the human town it was evening and many townsmen came out to stare suspiciously as they entered the center of town.

"Fear not. Your time of terror is over, the Great Wyrm of Orobas is slain!" Dorund said, and threw one of the sacks at the ground, gold coins spilling out with dramatic effect.

There were no immediate shouts of joy or victory. Instead, the people just blinked, confused, as if they were in disbelief.

"Is it true?" one man asked Alec.

"Yes, it is true."

Gradually the joy built as the reality set in. Many more people had arrived and the crowd buzzed with excitement. Men slapped Alec on the back and offered him strong drinks. To be polite he sampled what was given, but he was careful not to drink much. They were invited to stay the night at the Inn and given a hastily prepared but grand meal.

The next morning they were given new horses and plenty of provision to last the rest of the journey. Alec convinced Dorund to ride the pony and their progress was swift.

The journey home was solemn and quiet at first, but on the second day Dorund began to recite aloud The Saga of King Gomrund – Dragon-slayer. Even though he exaggerated or made up some things, Alec was pleased and the days went by pleasantly.

At last they were back home at the West Bridge. Dorund smiled at Alec and said, "Farewell Alec, dragon-slayer."

"Farewell Dorund."

Alec removed the gem from the packs and headed straight for the jail. It was mid afternoon and most in town were working in the fields. Brent was at the jail standing guard and let Alec into the cell.

Aldith's eyes were wide with wonder as Alec held up the glowing gem. "What do we do?"

Hesitantly, Aldith reached out, her fingers trembling. When she touched the gem, the milky flowing substance inside flashed for an instant then ran up her arm and into her chest. She lurched backwards, stunned, as if struck by lightning, then fell back into the cot.

"Aldith!" Liam screamed and dropped the gem, which clattered harmlessly to the ground. He held her in his arms and called her name. In a moment she opened her eyes and smiled weakly. Liam could see a subtle difference in her eyes, as if it were someone else there.

"Is my father...?"

"Yes, I'm sorry."

She began to weep, not only for her father, but for all of the people she harmed during her curse. Still on the ground she grabbed Alec's ankles and began speaking in a very soft voice.

Alec bent down, "What's wrong? What are you saying?"

She said, a little louder, "Forgive me." This she kept repeating. Her head was angled down. She would not look at him.

"For what? Attacking Nessa? That was not your fault."

She looked up, shaking her head. Her blue eyes were red from the tears.

"For what then?" Alec felt a sinking feeling in his chest, like he held a king's ransom in gold but it was flowing through his fingers and there was nothing he could do about it.

"Lying to you. Manipulating you. Getting you to kill my father."

"But I didn't. He was just knocked out." During the quest he imagined this moment in his mind many times, but it was never like this. He couldn't understand why she was upset and was beginning to be annoyed with her reaction.

By this time word had spread that Liam had returned and Brent, Galvin, and several other villagers rushed into the cell. They stopped and took in the scene. No one doubted that Aldith was cured, and she was allowed to leave with Liam.

A knock came on the cottage door followed quickly by an urgent shout, "Miss Wyn!"

Julia came to the top of the stairs and listened.

Wyn opened the door and a male voice said, "It's Cait, she took ill."

"How long?" Wyn asked.

"Just this morning, it was real sudden."

Wyn took her medicine bag and shouted up to the children, "I am going to the Millers. I will be back in two hours."

From her window Julia watched her mother disappear into the woods, then she burst into action. The faerie queen had promised that their mother would be led away, and Julia must bring all the children with her, except Alec whom she knew would never comply, and whom the faerie queen considered lost anyway.

"Morris, I am bringing Nessa to be healed and you must help me carry her."

"What? Does mother know?"

She hesitated, tempted to lie, but then said, "No, she is too proud to ask someone else to help."

He frowned and looked down, uncertain of what to do.

"Do you want Nessa to be able to walk again?"

"Yes."

"Then help me. I cannot carry her myself. We will be back before mother returns."

Reluctantly, he helped pick Nessa out of bed and dropped her down through the floor while Julia caught her from the bottom.

They walked along the river, taking turns carrying their sister, then reached the faerie bridge. Morris froze. Nessa was tame as a kitten, seeming to have lost her spirit with the injury although she claimed she could not remember the attack.

"Come on."

"Mother told us to never cross this bridge," Morris objected.

"This is an emergency. Who else could cure Nessa but the faeries?"

"How do you know they will help her?"

"Because the queen told me and she is our grandmother and wouldn't lie to us."

Julia marched on, knowing Morris would follow. He did and they crossed the bridge.

A few paces into the woods they were met by three handsome young elves. One smiled and said, "Greetings from the queen. She has sent us to fetch you home."

They took Nessa onto a palette they carried and led the children to the palace of the faerie queen.

Wyn returned from the Millers puzzled. The fever was strange with no other symptoms. She suspected witchcraft but didn't reveal this to the Millers. She prepared a potion she said was for fever but was actually an antidote to curses. Within fifteen minutes Cait had recovered to the Miller's surprise and delight. Wyn refused payment and hurried home, suddenly very worried.

The empty cottage indicated her greatest fear was true. She collapsed and began to sob. Her grief was followed by anger and she rushed out of the cottage, heading for the river.

She found Brogan in his cave in bear form.

"It has happened!"

Wyn and Brogan crossed the faerie bridge, heading for the palace. The crystal spires of the palace rose up in front of them about 200 yards away. Then suddenly, she stopped as if she had bumped into an invisible wall. She screamed and beat her hands against it. Brogan tried too but also failed. The queen had cast a powerful ward on the entire palace and she was powerless to break it. Wyn stepped back and tried a spell on the ward. There was a great booming noise but nothing else happened.

Wyn and Brogan sat on a rock by the river.

"At least we know they are safe," Brogan said.

"Safe? You do not know her as I do. She will bewitch them with magical means or not and soon they will all hate us as Julia now does."

"Surely she doesn't hate us, not truly."

"She said as much. She thinks it was my foolishness that exiled us."

"All children her age hate their parents, it is nature's way of assisting in the weaning process."

"I cannot rest until we get them back."

"I know."

"It must be on Samhain night."

"But that is when faeries are at the height of their power," Brogan said.

"Perhaps, but it's also when their weaknesses come to the fore."

"You have a plan?"

"Yes but I need help."

"The knight?"

"Just so."

"Will he help?"

"I can be very persuasive."

"Yes I know."

They smiled and held each other.

Time passed.

Brogan's eyes clouded and he said, "You best go now."

Julia was in one of the towers and heard the noise. Looking out she saw her father and mother and saw their despair. Her heart broke for them, but then the faerie queen summoned her and she was forced to leave the window.

Word spreads quickly through a little village, and soon Terrell heard that the children had been taken by the faerie queen. He also knew that Wyn had displayed terrible power on the night of the solstice, and judged she would be an excellent ally.

Terrell came to the cottage. The door was open and Wyn was inside, so deep in thought that she didn't see him standing there until he made a noise with his throat.

"I heard about your children. You have my deepest sympathy."

She said nothing.

"I have given Liam, the changeling boy, my protection, but I fear I may not be strong enough to thwart the faerie queen."

"Do not fear, you are not."

"Then help me. Perhaps together we can defeat her."

She looked up at Terrell and her eyes seemed to clear, as if she had woken from a dream.

"Yes, perhaps we can."

Visit to the Past

"I was just a young girl when my father, the king, died. An army of trolls invaded the land and killed the faerie king and his chief general Obryn. The queen claimed she had to make a pact with Cernunnos to help defeat the trolls. That is what I was told but we must find out exactly what happened the night the castle was destroyed," Wyn said.

"I already know what happened. I was there in my dream. The faerie king attacked with an army of trolls. When I woke the next morning I had a head wound from them," said Terrell.

"It wasn't just a dream, nor was it what really happened. There is more to this than meets the eye."

"How can we find out then?"

Wyn only smiled.

Wyn had spent the entire day preparing her spell. Unlike the foul and base magic of the witch, elf magic did not require the skin of babies, the eye of a newt, or the foam from a rabid dog. But she did need to rest, meditate, and clear her mind of all else. By evening, she was ready.

She and Terrell met at the castle. Terrell led her up to a small dressing room in the upper quarters of the castle that was sealed off by rubble until the recent renovations. On one of the walls was a full length mirror, cloudy but intact, and in the same position as it would have been centuries ago.

"You must only observe. Do not try to interfere or change what must again happen, or there will be terrible consequences," Wyn warned.

Terrell nodded.

"Now, eat this." Wyn handed Terrell some type of berry he had never before seen.

He obeyed, swallowing it down whole. Wyn stood and watched him closely.

"Now what?" Terrell said.

An instant later, Terrell was a cat, a small, brown and white one. The cat cautiously walked up to the mirror and observed itself, moving its head in order to see itself from different angles.

"It will be easier for you to watch unobserved in this form."

Terrell turned and stared at Wyn.

"Remember, when you are ready to return, come back through the mirror. Don't dally there too long or you may forget that you are human."

Wyn began the spell. It was an intricate performance involving chanting and precise body movements. Terrell could feel the power gather in the room. His scalp tingled and he could smell petrichor as if a thunderstorm were about to come. Then, suddenly, Wyn motioned toward the mirror and they could feel the power being released. The mirror clouded as if reflecting smoke.

Wyn's head was down and she was visibly exhausted. "Now! Jump into the mirror."

Terrell looked at Wyn, hesitated for a moment, then with one graceful bound, jumped into and through the mirror, disappearing into the haze.

He landed back in the same room, only the room was subtly different. It was cleaner. A fresh coat of whitewash was on the walls and brightly colored female clothing was strewn across the room. There was a large dresser against the far wall which was not there in the future. Terrell turned back to look at the mirror. It looked shiny and new. There was no smoke. He felt a fleeting feeling of panic, wondering if somehow the spell had failed and there would be no way to return, but this quickly passed as his faith in Wyn's magic was strong.

The door was ajar and he peeked into the bedroom. It was very dark. Someone was in the bed. He jumped on to the bed, landing as softly as a butterfly. It was her! Rowena was there sleeping. He watched her for a time and without realizing it, or how he was doing it, began to purr. Nestling beside her, he sat and watched for hours until finally falling asleep.

"Oh, what a darling cat!" she said.

Terrell awakened. It was morning. Rowena was petting him. He purred and rolled over on his back. He was in bliss as she petted and spoke lovingly to him.

"Where have you come from? Well, I suppose you are mine now. What shall I call you? Hmm how about Hermes? Yes, I shall call you Hermes."

Terrell wished he could speak to her but was content to at least be with her in the flesh.

Later in the morning she dressed and went down to the kitchens to find breakfast. He followed her closely, often rubbing against her legs. She grabbed some fruit and a roll from the pantry and asked one of the servants to fetch some cold fish for Hermes. To his relief it was cooked and he ate it gratefully.

She went into the garden to sit in the shade. Terrell could hardly believe how the castle looked. Everything was brand new and shining. It was obvious the castle was only recently completed. In fact, he noticed that there was ongoing work on the outer wall. It occurred to him that the wall must have never been completed which is why so little of it was left in his time.

A boy ran over to them from the castle. He was a few years younger than Rowena and he realized this must be her brother.

"Eirwyn! See my new pet? He was in my bed this morning

when I woke up. Isn't he darling?"

"What's his name?" Eirwyn sat beside them and petted the cat who was on her lap.

"Hermes."

They decided to go explore the countryside. Terrell gleaned they moved to the castle only days ago. They packed some food into a basket and went to the stables where two small horses were prepared.

Rowena mounted hers and said to Hermes, "You wait here my love. I will be back in the evening."

Eirwyn snickered.

Hermes made a mighty jump and scrambled up the saddle, then nestled in between her legs. "Oh!" she laughed. "Very well, you shall come too."

They rode by a man of middle age with a beard and long white hair.

"Bye Father. We are going on a picnic."

He smiled and waved.

They rode through the castle gatehouse down the road leading to town. The overgrown and decrepit orchard of his day was now tidy and well kept in neat even rows. The road was free of ruts and weeds. They passed into the town. He noticed some buildings from his day were gone but all were well kept. Many villagers were out and about who smiled and waved at the prince and princess.

They passed into the main street and Terrell could see the row of houses that were in ruins in the future were bright and newly built. They passed over the east bridge and continued south west along the road. Terrell knew they were heading into faerie territory and was tempted to try to warn her, but remembered what Wyn said about interfering.

They passed into rolling green hills and made camp at the top of one. There were wildflowers all over and Rowena picked a handful. She laid out a blanket and they sat on it, all three of them falling fast asleep.

Terrell was awakened by the sound of an approaching horse. Terrell tried to speak, but a meow was all that he could manage. This did the trick, however, as Rowena awoke.

The rider was young and richly dressed, and had the confident look of a king.

"Who gave you leave to make camp on my land and pick my flowers?" he said.

"This land belongs to my father, the king, and I need not ask your leave," she answered angrily.

He smiled and he dismounted. "Your town exists only by my generosity and good favor."

"You say you are a king but I know from maps there are no other towns or castles in this region."

The king cast a quick spell, motioning to his right, and in the distance where there were once rolling green hills, there was now a grand palace; a busy cluster of tall towers, all round, and topped with a blue apse which rose to a sharp point. The masonry was a shiny, white stone which glimmered in the light. The magnificence of the structure made the Bunwych castle look humble by comparison.

...there was now a grand palace; a busy cluster of tall towers, all round, and topped with a blue apse which rose to a sharp point.

"I am the King of Elfhame, at your service," he bowed.

"Elfhame? I have never heard of that, and my tutor is an expert in geography," Eirwyn said, with awe in his voice.

"Then your tutor is a fool," said the king with humor.

"We must go now," Rowena said, frightened by the display of magic.

"Nay, tarry a while," commanded the king, who dismounted and walked closer to her.

Terrell arched his back and hissed.

"That is an unusual cat," he said, stopping, his eyes narrowing in curiosity. Terrell felt exposed, feeling that somehow the king knew his true nature.

"We must!" Rowena said again, gathering the things and rushing to her horse.

"The tournament is tomorrow. Will you come?" Eirwyn said.

This seemed to placate the king, who smiled and said, "I will."

The prince and princess rode off, Eirwyn looking back and waving. Rowena kissed the cat and said, "My brave lion, how you protect me."

The royal children rode home and spent the rest of the day watching preparations for the celebrations. Terrell was pampered, given milk then raw chicken, which he would not eat, some cooked meat was offered later, which he did eat.

A large flat pasture north of the castle had been cleared for the tournament. The lists were the quadrangular field of battle which was longer than broad by one fourth. They were enclosed by a double row of palisade, five feet high; high enough to make it impossible for the horse to leap over. The space between the rows affording a place of refuge for the varlets and attendants. A thick covering of sand was strewn on the ground, so as to provide a cushion to falling knights. The lists were gaily decorated with bunting and pendants from the attending knights. Wooden bleachers were being constructed which overlooked the battle field.

By nightfall the castle was still bustling with activity but the prince and princess were ordered to bed.

At dawn, Terrell woke and looked out the window. The transformation of the grounds was spectacular. Brightly colored pavilions numbering in the hundreds surrounded the field of battle. Many different kingdoms were represented as indicated by the vast assortment of pendants flying from the tents. The bleachers were completed. The balcony was roofed with a blue fabric and hanging from the sides were tapestries showing the royal coat of arms which was a unicorn against a blue background.

Rowena was dressed in a fine dress of light blue color. To his relief, Rowena brought Terrell to the tournament, secreting him in a wicker basket and having a servant carry him over. The festivities began with a pageant in which the nobility, which numbered near one hundred, rode through the lists in their finest regalia, amidst genuine cheering and applause from the spectators.

The highest seats were reserved for the nobles and a balcony where the royal coterie was seated. The commoners stood on the level of the lists and would be forced to see as well as they could. The cavaliers wore equipment which differed in quality and embellishment, although all wore full plate. The horses were also embellished with bells hanging as neck-lets.

The first sport, which took up the entire morning, was called the Passage of Arms. A mock fortress was constructed within the lists out of wood. Two armies were formed, one, the Tenans, were tasked to defend the castle, and their foe, the Venans, were the attackers. The combatants fought with blunted swords. If a knight were disarmed or fell to the ground, he was captured. After an hour the Venans won the day and were applauded by the crowd.

In the afternoon was the melee, a hand to hand free for all with blunted swords and axes. It began with some twenty participants. They fought hard and much blood was spilled, although no one seemed to be seriously injured. At the end a tall man with dark gray armor was victorious and the king congratulated him.

The only game that remained was the jousting and Terrell was relieved the faerie king had not arrived. The tilt was constructed, which was a long fence in the middle of the lists which separated the two jousters.

There was a commotion from outside the battlefield, a disturbance in the crowd. The crowd parted and a man rode into the lists on a white horse. He was finely dressed, but the style was unusual and slightly archaic. There was a murmur through the crowd. He rode up in front of the royal box and grinned.

Rowena said, "Father, may I present the King of Elfhame."

"Elfhame. Yes, my children have told me about your fine castle. You are welcome," said the king.

"Am I too late to compete in the tournament?"

"Compete?" The king said, confused. There was laughter in the crowd. "But where is your armor, your helm?"

If the faerie king was bothered by the laughter he didn't show it. He lifted up his fine, green, velvet doublet and chain mail glinted from underneath. "I brought no lances, however. May I borrow one?"

"Yes, of course," the king said, still confused but accepting.

He rode a few more feet and faced Rowena, "May I carry

your favor?"

She blushed slightly, but took a silk veil down from her hat and threw it to him, which he caught deftly with his lance, tossed it up to his hand, and tied it around his shoulder. Terrell arched his back and hissed, but no one noticed. One of the attendants motioned to the faerie king and he followed to where the other combatants waited.

The horns sounded and the tournament had begun. On the field knights collected and combatants were organized by a gray haired man, the king's uncle.

First up were the faerie king and a knight with silver armor and a red banner.

The two combatants charged at full speed, lances up. The crowd was silent. No one breathed. They collided and the rider in the silver armor was thrown, his lance glancing off the faerie king's shield. He was victorious. The crowd murmured in appreciation.

Another jouster challenged him and another career was started. Again, the King of Elfhame was victorious, throwing his opponent and not even shifting in his seat.

A dozen other challengers tried their fortune against him, but all were defeated, and he always kept his seat. Some courses were won by points, but most won by unhorsing his opponent.

After the supply of challengers were exhausted, the Golden Knight rode up to the royal seats.

"A superb display of skill. I commend you," said the king good-naturedly.

"I would like to claim my prize," said the faerie king.

"Prize? Why there are no prizes in this tournament. It is for amusement only." The king turned to his adviser, whispering, "There are no prizes, yes?" His adviser nodded in agreement.

The faerie king looked over to the princess and smiled.

She blushed.

The king noticed and said, "Ah I understand. Well, the prize may be granted by the princess at her own discretion." He waved in the air as if he cared not a drop although in his heart he was both glad for the attention being paid to his daughter and wistful knowing his daughter will someday soon be taken from him by a marriage.

Terrell felt like vomiting a hairball.

Rowena smiled shyly and blew the Golden Knight a kiss.

"Is that all?"

"And I will grant you the first dance at the ball," she added.

"A prize worth a hundred kingdoms. I am content. Until tonight." He bowed and rode off.

The faerie king's courting of Rowena must be part of the puzzle, he knew, but he could not fathom what it meant. He was being driven mad by the fact that she seemed to welcome the attention.

If the ball was tomorrow night, time was running out. Terrell realized if he were to obtain any useful information, he must go to Elfhame. So with great regret, he left Rowena and the castle.

Terrell walked through town as the sun set, once having to run and jump over a fence to avoid a dog. He crossed the faerie bridge and came through the forest to the rolling hillsides. The faerie palace rose up in the distance, the sunset gleaming gold and red off the shiny surface of the towers.

By the time Terrell reached the castle entrance it was quite dark out. The gates were closed but there was ivy climbing up the walls and it was easy for him to climb up and through a window. He found himself in a long corridor. A young elf maiden who looked to be five by human standards saw him and froze, unaccustomed to seeing a cat in the palace. She looked oddly familiar. Both stared at each other for a few moments until a voice called out, "Aethelwyne! Come this instant!" and she ran off. This was Wyn as a child he realized.

He kept moving, looking and listening for a sign of the king or queen.

At last, Terrell heard his voice. He was coming toward him. He jumped up on a window and hid in the dark sill while the king passed by, moving quickly.

...cluttered with scrolls, books, flasks, wands, baskets, maps, crystals, skulls, bones, candles, stuffed animals, and a thousand other esoteric items.

The faerie king climbed one of the smaller but higher towers in the palace. Terrell followed, keeping just out of sight. They came to a circular room, cluttered with scrolls, books, flasks, wands, baskets, maps, crystals, skulls, bones, candles, stuffed animals, and a thousand other esoteric items. Terrell hid behind some crates.

Sitting there at a desk was a tiny, wizened looking elf with a small, pointed beard white as chalk.

"What can I do for you, Your Highness?"

"A simple love spell is all," said the king.

"A potion?"

"No. An incantation."

"For that you must have a strand of hair from the-"

The king pulled out a silk veil with a flourish. It was the favor given to him by Rowena. The wizard squinted at the cloth and took it.

"It will be done by the evening."

"Very good," said the king, who quickly left the room.

Hatred and jealousy burned in Terrell's heart. He watched the magician, trying to think of a way to stop him. In a few moments, the old faerie's head tipped back and a loud snoring ensued. An idea came to Terrell and he rushed out of the room. He went down to the lower levels and scanned the floor carefully as he walked. There! He found one. He took the hair in his mouth and rushed back up to the wizard's room.

The wizard was still asleep and Terrell jumped up on the desk and replaced Rowena's hair with the one he found. With joy in his heart, Terrell climbed into an empty basket and slept soundly.

He was awakened the next morning by heavy footsteps echoing from the stairwell down. The faerie king burst into the room and shouted, "What have you done you old fool!?"

The wizard woke with a startled cry, looking up at the king with watery eyes, "How may I serve you my Lord?"

"The spell! It has gone wrong. During the night one of the horses in the stable went mad! It broke loose and came to my bedchamber! It tried to molest me."

If Terrell could have laughed, he would. His selection of a hair could not have been planned better.

"I am sorry my Lord. I don't see how this could have happened. Would you like me to try again?"

"No! You have done enough. I do not need magical help any way." He stormed out of the room.

Terrell was not finding any information of value. He knew the queen was the key to everything and decided to watch her closely. He found her chambers and was able to enter without being seen. Quickly he dashed under the bed, passing through silky sheets which hid him but still let him observe.

The king entered. His dress was flamboyant. His costume for the ball? Terrell wondered. The queen entered and faced him.

"You choose the company of humans over faeries on this of all nights?" she said with contempt.

"Your cold heart blows me away like a November gale," he said with the tone of mourning something long gone.

"If I have a cold heart, you have none at all," said the queen.

"If my heart is cold, yours is lost."

"How can you consort with men as if they were our equals? Remember you are the leader of our people. It demeans us," she said.

"They have certain charms. Perhaps you could learn a thing or two from their fellowship."

"Learn what? How to wage war and lay to waste your own lands."

"Our people make war too. We have in the past had kinship with the humans, remember?"

"Yes, and always to our regret," she said. "They are filthy savages. They have no culture, no art."

"They have music and poetry. Not so different from our race when it was young." The king touched her shoulder tenderly. "She is a mere plaything. Why do you fret? Do you think so little of yourself?"

Her face was bright with jealousy, "And who will I dance with tonight? You would humiliate me for a tryst. Do not go."

"I shall go as I have promised."

"Go to her then! I will find another to dance with, perhaps Lord Orbryn."

There was a pause of two heartbeats when all stood still and the royal couple glared at each other. Then, with the swiftness of a snake, the king pushed her against the wall and drew his razor thin dirk, holding it against her throat.

"So, the rumors are true. You have taken my chief adviser for your lover?"

"No! It was only a threat! Just words." Her eyes were now white with fear.

Orbryn rushed into the room, sword drawn. "Release her."

The king released the queen, threw down his dagger, and drew his own sword. "You would draw your sword on your own king?" He said this not with anger but with disgust and contempt.

"It was fated," Orbryn said, mysteriously.

The swordplay was so quick the blades were a blur. The battle was fierce and quick. The king wounded Orbryn in the arm, then with the next stroke, pierced him through the heart.

The queen rushed to him. "You killed him!"

"No my queen, you killed him. He was a better man than you deserved. Count your blessings tonight and consider what you have sewn." He sheathed his sword and left the room, his cape fluttering behind.

She held up the head of Orbryn, who was already cold. "I will avenge you. He can't do this to me," she said but with no tears, only rage.

She rushed out of the room. Terrell followed.

He followed her into a thick wood. The trees were ancient. A thick carpet of moss covered the bark.

There was a thin trickling brook which she followed upstream. The brook widened and led into a green, shady grotto. The queen pulled up her skirt and waded into the cold, ankle deep water, disappearing into the darkness.

Terrell stopped there a while, an unnatural fear of the water suddenly taking hold. He shook this off and followed into the cave, picking a route along the edge which kept him mostly dry. He could hear voices inside and saw the faerie queen kneeling before a creature which had the head of a deer and body of a man with green leaves covering its body like hair. It was seven feet tall, not including its enormous antlers; twelve pointed like a stag.

Behind the creature was a rock face where the spring welled from. The cave was moist and verdant but there was no trace of decay or mold in the air.

"Why do you summon me?" the creature asked. Its voice was vigorous and resonant, but not malevolent."

"Cernunnos, Great Lord of the Forest, I beg thee, grant me a boon." She bowed low, then continued, "the faerie king has gone mad. He has killed another faerie and means to take a human girl for a bride."

"What concern is that of mine?"

"The balance of nature is disturbed. He favors a human tribe which will infest this land and lay it to waste. Grant me an army that I can use to defeat him and restore things to their rightful state."

"There will be a cost," he stated.

"I will pay it," she answered without hesitation.

There was no sound but the trickling of water for several moments.

At last Cernunnos spoke, "Go to the standing stones, there you will find your army. For this you are forever indebted. Every seven years you are bound to pay a tithe. Leave one of your people there on the night of Samhain. Fail this tribute at your own peril."

Terrell closed his eyes so that the queen could not see his glowing irises as she passed. When he opened them the horned creature was gone. He left the cave and made for the dawns maidens.

The half moon was now risen, alighting the rolling hills in a pale glow. Terrell could see the shapes of the standing stones in the distance and the still silhouette of the queen in their midst. She moved and then there was the sound as if a hundred millstones were turning, and the stones themselves seemed to move and shift. He ran to get closer. Each of the thirteen groups of stones were composed of two vertical stones and one cap stone placed atop the other two. The stones were changing, transforming as he watched. The vertical stones became legs, and the cap stone grew into a torso, a rough head, and two huge arms. They stopped contorting and became still, watching the queen as if waiting for orders.

"I command you! Cross the river and march to the human castle. Kill the faerie king. Kill everyone there. Destroy the castle.

Now go!" She pointed violently at the castle far in the distance.

Terrell could feel the ground shake as the ponderous army marched forward. He ran with desperate urgency. He must somehow warn Rowena, his promise not to interfere a dim memory now. The stone giants moved slowly but covered much ground with each step. By the time he reached the faerie bridge they were already crossing the river. Heart pounding, he forced himself onward; cats were not good distance runners.

The faerie queen watched her army march, the feeling of power was intoxicating. For so long she ruled in the shadow of the king. Now she held command and would wield it mercilessly, making sure her people remained separate and hidden from mankind.

A slender figure appeared on the now strangely barren hill. It was Maeraedeth, but now youthful in appearance.

"Do not take this path. Call them back before it is too late!"

"It is too late," the queen spat.

Maeraedeth's eyes began to glimmer. Power was welling inside her. The queen took a stride toward her and went into a fighting stance. Electricity crackled and the air took on a metallic smell as awesome magic was gathering. Suddenly a white orb of pure power rose from Masquerader's (did you mean Maeraedeth?) palm and shot out, but the queen quickly raised her hand and the orb was halted, suspended between the two faeries, hovering in mid air. The battle continued in a stalemate; their faces grim with concentration, each trying to harness the uttermost power.

Then, Maeraedeth faltered. A subtle look of doubt flashed on her face. The queen smiled and the orb shot back toward Maeraedeth, striking her and blasting her away like a bolt of lightning. She landed at the bottom of the hill, not dead but unconscious, all her power drained and her faerie imbued youth gone forever. The queen strode to her and looked down calmly. Maeraedeth regained consciousness and looked up at her enemy.

"No, I will not slay you, but you will be cast out to live with the goblins, and I place on you a geas. You shall not speak of this night to another soul for as long as you shall live."

When Terrell reached the town center he knew it was too late. Already he could hear the terrible sounds of destruction; rock crushing against rock mingled with screams of men and women and the occasional terrified whinny of a horse.

His heart was pounding from the run and he felt strange, light headed, as if he were watching everything from a distance. A group of people ran by, fleeing the castle in his direction. They were all servants, eyes wide with terror. He hid in the shadow of a building as they passed, wanting only to hide, but he gathered his courage and forced himself on.

Passing by the orchard he could now see the castle and the shapes of the giant army against the star filled sky. The creatures had surrounded the castle and were smashing it with their massive fists of rock. He got into the bailey and circled around to the ballroom. Several fires had broken out. The ball room was completely destroyed and the army had moved on to other parts of the keep. He went in through the outer doors which were burst open. The ground was littered with bodies, their gay ball dress incongruous against the rubble floor. He wound through, sometimes leaping over the corpses, scanning for Rowena. In the center of the room he saw the faerie king. His face was pulverized but he recognized his colorful costume.

The smoke was thick but Terrell's low posture kept him out of the worst of it. Most of the lights were extinguished and the air was cloudy with dust. He could hear the deep rumbles and explosions of the castle collapsing all around him.

Then he saw her. She was in the corner, her bright blue dress half buried in the gray rubble. He stared for a moment, his mind lost in a haze of sadness, but not fully comprehending. A great block of stone fell with a mighty crash just feet away. He darted off, animal instinct now taking over, wanting only to hide.

One last shred of human intellect drove him through the castle into the royal quarters. The mirror was still there, intact, but cloudy, as it had been when the spell was first cast. He leaped into it.

Mere seconds after he had disappeared through the mirror (from the point of view of Wyn) the cat returned, leaping out of the mirror and into the room, collapsing immediately on the ground and gasping for air. Without hesitation, Wyn cast the counter spell to return Terrell to his human shape. He lay there for a time, exhausted, while she waited impatiently. Wyn gave him some water. Finally, he regained his wind and recounted everything he had seen.

A plan was made and Wyn returned home. Terrell retired to his room, exhausted but too troubled to sleep. He had witnessed the death of his love twice in as many days. But was she really his love? How well did he really know Rowena? His dream from the night before had not really happened. Was that an illusion? Was it all illusion?

Morris was finding the glamor and pomp of the palace too saccharine and began sneaking out and walking into the hills overlooking Bunwych. He missed his mother terribly but feared the faerie queen too much to ask to go back. The food was rich and sweet yet somehow not nourishing. He longed for some simple homemade oatmeal.

Julia, however, was enamored by the palace, so clean and bright. She loved the fine clothes, the delicate food, and bathing every night in the luxurious bathrooms in the palace. The largest was a chamber open to the air. Pillars along the sides held up the walls, up which green vines climbed. The water was about hip deep and always warm, no matter the season. The heady aroma of flowers from the nearby gardens filled the air.

The children were required to attend school, tutored by the wizard Rhyllgallohyr. There were five other elfin children in the classroom, and the three half human children were far behind them. Morris felt stupid. The other children were cruel and teased the half human children mercilessly. Morris ran off as much as he could although he was punished. Punishment took the form of whipping with a chord, or being forced to drink a bright green elixir which made Morris sick to his stomach.

Nessa was having a bad night. She was tired and cranky from the rigid schedule and demands given to a royal child.

The children were minded by an older elf lady, Kelerandri, who was kind enough in a cold faerie way, but could sometimes also be harsh.

Nessa had just bathed and her attendant was trying to get her to put on her ball dress but she was tired and in a mood and a tantrum was about to begin.

"I don't want to dance tonight!" she screamed.

"You must!" Kelerandri stated.

"No!" She screamed.

The faerie queen entered the room and glared at Nessa, who shrank back.

"Enough!" the faerie queen said and motioned to Nessa. Immediately her throat closed up and she found she could no longer make a sound. This frightened her immensely and she collapsed into a ball on the floor soundlessly whimpering.

Julia rushed over to her and tried to comfort her.

The next morning the queen summoned Nessa and Morris. She was happy and pleasant and told them she had a surprise. She led them to the faerie stables to a clean stall with fresh, fragrant hay. There, curled up in the nest of hay, was a small white creature. Nessa gasped and said, "Unicorn!"

"Not just a unicorn, but the rarest of the rare, a baby one."

It was about the same size as a newborn horse. It had white fur and curiously, brown spots all over it. Its horn was but a finger's length and translucent. It opened its blue eyes and made a sound so endearing it made Nessa coo like a morning dove.

She crouched down closer to it. "May I touch it?" she asked reverently.

"Of course, it is yours," the queen answered.

"Mine?"

"Yes, you and your brother must share."

"It has spots like a young deer," Morris said.

"Yes, and like a fawn, the spots will go away when it grows up. If I give you this creature you must make a vow to care for it. It shall need to be hand fed every morning and night. Do you promise?"

"With all my heart!" Nessa answered.

"Morris?"

"I promise," he answered.

"Remember, the bond between a unicorn fawn and its parents are uncommonly strong. If you fail in your duties it will perish."

Millard accepted Terrell's kind offer to stay in the castle while Liam was still in danger. A wing on the first floor of the castle, which was once the servants quarters, had been reconstructed by the goblins and was quite suitable to their purposes, although it needed a great amount of cleaning and other work to make it truly livable.

Millard was busy building a rough table that would serve as a dinner table while the females of the house were cleaning. Liam had just brought in a load of wood and was resting as his sister Elinor returned from the river carrying a basket of washed clothes. He suddenly became quite pale as he watched her enter the room with his other sister and mother. As a benefit of living with the goblins for so long Liam had the gift of faerie sight so could see that it was not his sister that had returned from the river but a goblin enchanted to look like his sister.

She gave a sly glance at him as she passed with another load, heading back to the river. "I will help you, Elinor."

Millard smiled watching them, pleased that his family was finally reunited and the seed of discord which was false Liam was gone.

At the river, past the sight of his family Liam asked, "Where is she?"

"Safe. Come with me and you will see," it answered.

"Will you give me your word she will be released if I come?"

"Yes, we have no need for her. You are one of us. Come back to us. Come back home."

Reluctantly, and not trusting the goblin, Liam felt he had no choice and followed the goblin back to Elfhame.

After an hour, when Liam and Elinor had not returned from the river, Millard had alerted Terrell and a search party was in the process of being formed. That was when Elinor returned, shaken and confused. Most of her memory of the incident was gone but she had fleeting visions of goblins and their coarse fingers grabbing her.

Inside the burrow was a huge earthen chamber with roots dangling from the ceiling. The huge chamber was filled with garbage and items stolen from the village. Goblins are good builders but as shown by Dozank and Galvin's other goblins, they are slovenly and what they build soon crumbles and decays. There was a horse carriage, overturned to make a good sized house for the small goblins. Goblins were strewn about everywhere, many sleeping, ramshackle.

This goblin burrow was better than the village of huts where Liam used to live, for this was where aristocracy of the goblins lived. But like human aristocracy often is, they tended to be cruel and selfish.

Liam was in a small cage made of wicker branches wound together tightly with sturdy twine. It was too small for him to stand up but he could lay down flat.

Seeing he was awake, the goblin king came over, grinning. "For taking you the faerie queen gave us ten barrels of beer!" He looked about, "Here's to the changeling returned to us!" The goblins around him cheered and toasted as Liam looked on from his cage miserably.

As the night wore on the goblin lair became more noisy and rowdy. Many were drunk and singing. Often a goblin would walk by his cage or scowl at the boy or mutter something like "Changeling don't get too comfortable." A particularly drunk goblin came over and offered the boy his cup, then pulled it away when he reached for it.

Later, a tiny goblin boy crept over to the back side of his cage and stared solemnly for a long time. Finally Liam said, "Hello, I am Liam." He became scared and dashed away as quick as a mouse. Soon, he returned though, this time bearing a glass cup. Shyly, he offered it to Liam. It was water and he was grateful. "Thanks," he said, but then a female goblin cried "Ratskin!" and the goblin boy scurried away again.

Gradually the noise abated as the goblins in turn fell asleep or passed out and Liam was able to fall asleep on his bed of straw.

He tried to pry apart the wicker bars but they were too sturdy. If he only had something to cut with, he could surely cut through the bindings. In a flash Liam had an idea. He took the glass cup, and quietly as he could, smashed it against the ground.

It did not break. He tried again, harder and finally it shattered into several pieces, cutting his hand but not badly. Hearing a noise, he quickly covered the shards with straw. A goblin came over and peered inside, but seeing nothing, left.

Liam waited several more hours till there was not a stirring or sound except the snoring of the goblins which all of them seemed to do.

He sawed through the chords and soon loosened a spot large enough to squeeze through. Slipping out of the cage as quietly as possible, he picked a path through the rubbish toward the exit. He had to creep so closely to a goblin that he could smell its foul breath, but it didn't awaken. He was just a few yards from the door when two burly goblins jumped out from the darkness. They had clubs and struck Liam multiple times with cruel but non lethal blows to his body. Grabbing him roughly, they thrust him back in the cage, after first repairing the damage and cleaning out all of the glass.

Just then, at his lowest point, he heard a voice, "Liam." It was Wyn.

He looked about. "Where are you?" he whispered.

"I am not there with you but I will come to free you soon. Where are you being held?"

"Under the goblin hill where the goblin king lives."

"Fear not Liam, I will free you soon. I promise."

Wyn and Terrell stepped through the door and Terrell was amazed to see a chamber much bigger than he expected or even thought was physically possible given its size from the outside. Hundreds of goblins were there cavorting and carousing in all manner of ramshackle structures. Atop a great hill of garbage was a shoddy throne on which sat the goblin king. Terrell saw this immediately upon stepping into the kingdom but in exactly three seconds there was a great hush, as if one intruded into a noisy pond of bullfrogs and they all became instantly silent when they sensed him. Most of them ducking out of sight, some of the bolder ones staring. Lights were extinguished and the place became as dim as a moonless night.

Without hesitation or fear, Wyn walked toward the goblin king who glared down at her silently but bitterly. When she got close enough to speak without shouting she stopped and spoke to the king, "We have come to take back the boy."

"Leave him, Princess. He is one of us."

"He belongs here no more than a frog in a desert."

"We cannot let you take him. The faerie queen will punish us," the king said defiantly, but Terrell sensed a hint of fear. Goblins are not known for bravery but the king was here in the heart of his domain.

Wyn had no doubt that she could take the boy by force but wished to avoid any bloodshed, and so stood there thinking of a way to bargain for the boy.

Terrell sensed this and came upon a way to bargain for the boy and allow the king to save face. He conveyed the plan quietly to Wyn and she agreed.

"We will make a wager for him," she said to the king. "This human will compete with you in a contest to see who can stand the most goblin whiskey."

The king's eyes lit up. Despite their small size, goblins were renowned for their ability to hold their drink.

The king climbed down and a rough table was fashioned and the two sat opposed to each other. A bottle was brought and two glasses were produced, then filled. Without taking their eyes off each other, Terrell and the goblin king drank the contents at once. A goblin wearing a pointed hat called out, "One!" There were cheers all around.

Terrell thought the goblin whiskey was foul and it burned horribly but he was careful to not show a trace of emotion.

The night wore on and the goblin with the hat called out all the numbers through twenty, though he needed help once, forgetting the number seventeen. With each swallow the crowd gave a raucous cheer.

Terrell was terribly drunk but hardly showed it at all. The goblin king also seemed unchanged, which worried Wyn. She considered casting some kind of spell to help the knight, but could not think of one that could be cast undetected. She decided to try to distract the king instead.

"My congratulations on what you have done in your kingdom. It is more magnificent than I remember."

"Do you think so?"

"Indeed."

His speech was decidedly slurred. This gave Terrell hope.

The count reached thirty and both contestants were showing telltale signs of intoxication. In truth, it was the most drunk Terrell had ever been and he feared he could not continue much longer. The goblin king's eyes were by now most definitely crossed and he swayed to and fro on his chair to some unknown rhythm.

Terrell had an idea. He began to sway with the goblin, keeping his eyes locked with the goblin and increasing the speed and angle of the swaying with each movement. It was making Terrell nauseous but he was sure the goblin was worse off and continued, determined to win.

Cup number thirty one was emptied and the king swayed to the left, ending up on the floor, unconscious but with a happy grin on his face.

Wyn called out, "The contest is ours!" The goblins let out a chorus of boos and hisses. "Release the prisoner and bring him to us." She said this with such an air of authority that three goblins immediately jumped up and jostled with each other to get to the cage.

Terrell merely sat there, with eyes open and fixed into space, unable to move. Wyn came over and helped him up. He stood, wobbly and unbalanced with one arm around her. Liam joined them and helped Terrell on his other side. They left the goblin hill without incident.

They managed to get Terrell home but not before he purged himself on the bridge.

Terrell took Lyneth by the hand and led her into the castle. Suspense hung thick in the air. He told her nothing and in her mind he was leading her to a secret present. For him, however, this was a serious test. Many rooms in the living quarters were restored, although they still remained to be furnished. Terrell contracted with the town carpenter and although he had apprentices, the process would be slow.

They came to the gallery and stopped at the portrait of the long dead King Baglan. Terrell watched Lyneth carefully but there was no change in her vacant though happy expression. Next Queen Cordelia; again no change. At last they came to the portrait of Rowena. Despite the different dress and hair style, the two girls looked identical even down to the birthmark on her left cheek. Was there a slight flicker of recognition? Or was that just wishful thinking? He could not be sure.

"You and she look alike."

"Do you think so?" She was quite pleased, for she had never even seen such a fine dress, let alone wear one.

Terrell pulled out a hand mirror he had earlier placed against the wall and held it up to her. "The birthmark on your cheek, it is there on the painting, don't you see it?" His heart began to pound and without meaning to his voice rose in intensity. He could see Lyneth's eyes widen with fear.

"I'm sorry, my love. I don't know what came over me. Let me show you the rest of the rooms."

He showed her the royal suite, the library, the kitchen and buttery, and the ballroom which was still incomplete. Leading her out to the veranda overlooking the river, he took her hand and said, "Do you like it, my love?"

"Yes, it is beautiful and very grand."

"Would you be happy living here, my love?"

Her smile faded and she looked down, "Are you sure it is I

who you love and not the girl in the painting?"

He was stunned and at a loss for words. He gave her too little credit, not suspecting that she was so aware of his emotions. Perhaps she was right.

"When you are ready to decide, I will be waiting," she said with an understanding smile.

Terrell watched her go with a heavy heart.

Samhain

The autumn solstice, when the darker half of the year begins, is a liminal time when faeries, especially wicked ones, are at their height of power and can enter Bunwych freely. The villagers are wise enough to remain locked in their homes at night, leaving sprigs of pine or rowan on their doors, and burning bonfires during the day to keep the evil spirits at bay. Offerings of bread, wine, and other foods would be left out to appease the faeries. It was also considered to be a time when the souls of the dead could enter our world and revisit their kin.

During the day the villagers engage in a ritual called the Grey Bogy Procession in which they would dress in costume and go door to door throughout the town, blowing on horns, reciting verses, and singing songs. The procession had many players, the most important of which was the carrier of the skull, and was a great honor to be chosen in this role. This person carried the mare's skull attached to a pole, its eyes stuffed with colored wool, and bells dangled from its reins. A sheet covered the carrier and he would snap the jaw's of the skull together at passers by. Another important role was the Merryman, a kind of clown, a smartly dressed leader who would carry a whip and feign whipping passers by. The others in the procession would wear masks, usually based on an animal or monster.

Forty two villagers gathered in the village green in front of the clock tower. It was almost noon and the Grey Bogy Procession would start soon.

In recognition of his work in foiling the dwarf king's plot to marry the fair Lyneth, Galvin was chosen to play the carrier of the skull. He held the pole onto which the horses skull was attached. Its eyes were stuffed with bright, green wool. A white sheet was attached to the back of the skull and hung down over Galvin, disguising his identity although all in town knew it was him. He was pleased to play the carrier, especially since it meant he didn't have to sing.

Tomos was chosen to be leader and would lead Galvin, blinded by his sheet, by two reins attached to the front of the skull. He was smartly dressed in his finest black suit and also carried a whip which he would periodically snap with glee.

Nash, the miller, was chosen to be the Merryman, as he was for the past several years, for the main reason that he was the best fiddle player in the village. His face was garishly but gaily painted.

Kent, a boy of seventeen, played punch and carried a poker which he would tap on the ground to the music, or on doors, or other people.

Judy, complete with a wig of golden hay, was played by Alcott, who was fourteen. He carried a broom which he used to sweep the ground, or walls, doors, or people's backsides.

Also in the procession were about ten village children.

> Here we come,
> dear friends,
> to ask permission to sing.
>
> If we don't have permission,
> let us know in song
> how we should go away tonight.
>
> I have no dinner
> or money to spend
> to give you welcome tonight.

They went from house to house, singing and playing. The inhabitants of the house were meant to open the door and hand out beer or shots of liquor to the adults and sweets to the children.

When they came to the house of Kerwin, he came out and engaged in a rhyming contest with Tomos, and was defeated handily.

Samhain Night

In the castles tallest tower were Wyn, Terrell, Liam, Alec, Aldith, Millard, Bess, Elinor, and Kyla. Cushions were spread across the circular room and everyone was relaxed and comfortable. They barricaded the doors on every level and the long, narrow windows were too small for a man or goblin to fit through.

The faerie queen was terrible to behold. She rode a roan gray mare with glowing red eyes and wore elvish battle armor and held up a long, silver sword which gleamed in the pale moonlight. Behind her were dozens more elves, all males, all dressed for battle.

Riding with the elves were martes; dark elves which lived in the darkest swamps and forests, so terrible to behold that even Wyn was afraid.

"Don't worry. they can not get in," Terrell said.

"Come away from the windows. Do not look outside," Wyn said.

"Elinor, give us a song," said Bess.

She began singing and Millard joined in with his fiddle.

They circled the castle, riding swiftly; more swiftly than any mortal ever could.

A troll began to scale the tower wall, and upon reaching the window, began to take out bites of the stone with its terrible mouth. Elinor and Kyla screamed. Terrell pulled out his sword and thrust at the creature which tried to grab it. The enchanted blade bit through its hand and it slipped and fell with a mad cry.

Galvin paced in his library, repeatedly sipping a fine, vintage wine. He knew what night this was and how the dead return to dance in the starlight. His clock struck eleven and he turned to the clock, sweat beading on his temples. The wine was strong and he was quite intoxicated. At last, like a spring being released, he could no longer hold back and rushed through the door into the night.

In a mixture of terror and anticipation, he reached a pleasant meadow. It was where he and his love often met, many, many years ago. He stroked the bark of a tree where he had carved their initials. The tree had healed, leaving only a faint scar.

He felt something and turned. She was there, smiling. He took her hand, and although he could not feel her, they held hands and danced. There was no music. Yet, somehow, he heard music and they danced.

Time passed and Galvin knew she must soon depart from him again. But this time was different. He told her, "Go now, my love, but do not return. Rest instead in peace. My heart has healed like this tree. It is time I resumed my life."

She gazed at him at first with sadness, then smiled and simply drifted away.

At the castle a great pounding could now be heard, so loud that it made the very tower shake. Terrell rushed over to the window and looked down. There was a fearsome man-like creature the size of a bull, with long, shaggy hair, eyes like saucers, and impossibly long arms which it was using to bash down the door.

"It will break down the door. I must go down," Terrell said.

"No! That is what they want. Leave him to me," Wyn said. She grabbed the jug of water they were drinking from and walked over to the window. She passed her hand over the jug and said an incantation, then poured the water out of the window. The water multiplied tenfold and became like molten glass as it dripped over the boggarts back. It gave out a terrible cry and ran like a demon for the river.

"Well done," Terrell said.

Wyn smiled and said, "We shall need more water."

"I'll get it," Kyla said.

Still looking through the window, Wyn said, "The queen has gone. It is time for the royal banquet and she must attend."

"Is it over then?" Liam asked hopefully.

"No, but soon," she replied.

Kyla walked over to the well room, conveniently built to allow the royal inhabitants to pull from the well even at this high level. She pulled the ropes and the tin bucket came up. Reaching for it, she was given a start, because sitting on the edge was a small, green frog. Being a country girl, she had no fear and swatted at it, causing it to jump off and back into the well. Thinking nothing of it, she emptied the pail into the water jug and brought it back to the room where everyone was.

Everyone drank, and in ten minutes, all were sound asleep from drinking the enchanted water. The frog climbed back up the well, transformed back into a goblin, and opened the door to the tower.

Liam awoke realizing he was bound and a course sack was over his head.

He could not see but knew they were carrying him through town. Their feet echoed hollowly on the wooden planks as they carried him over the bridge. Thereupon it was up and down hills and through brush.

Then, finally he was put down and all was still.

"Untie him."

There was the faerie queen, now out of her armor and

dressed lavishly for the faerie banquet.

"You should not have run away. This is your destiny. It was why you were born. Fear not, it is a great honor to be taken by Cernunnos."

"Why don't you go with him then?"

"Silence." She waved her hand nonchalantly in front of him and he instantly lost the power of speech.

"Take him," she said, and walked away.

They took him to the dawn maidens, tying him securely to one of the stones and they left. It was forbidden to watch the ritual.

In the palace of the faeries, a great banquet was under way. The largest hall was filled with a tremendously long table set with a white, lace tablecloth. It was filled with the succulent food and drink of the faeries. There was music and merriment, and not a consideration given to the sacrifice that was taking place. An endless stream of goblin servants were serving dishes from silver trays.

At the dawns maidens the air became very still. The crickets ceased their chirping and the frogs their croaking. Cernunnos appeared between two of the stones. Liam's heart froze.

Cernunnos stood before the boy and regarded him. "What is this treachery? I am offered a common goblin with an illusion cast to make him look human." As he spoke the spell was broken and the boy was now a goblin.

Wyn emerged from the shadows and spoke, "You have been cheated lo these many years. The queen has been giving you humans who have lived as elves and eaten elven food, to give them the scent of an elf."

"The pact has been broken. Payment must be collected," Cernunnos stated without anger.

The forest god turned and walked towards the palace. Wyn followed.

The plan Wyn had devised was perfectly executed. Liam had bravely agreed to be retaken, but not until late in the night when the queen would be distracted by the banquet. Wyn feigned sleeping from the potion but had followed closely behind Liam as they took him back to Elfhame. At the last possible moment before midnight, when the guards had slipped away, she swapped false Liam back for the human boy, ensuring the anger of the horned god, and the breaking of the pact.

The atmosphere at the banquet was tense. The faerie queen was at the head of the table in a taller and more ornate chair than anyone else. Morris, Julia, and Nessa all sat together to her right, watching, and not speaking as if they expected something important to happen at any moment.

Suddenly a hush fell over the hall and a thick fog bellowed in from the open door at the hall entrance. All eyes turned to see Cernunnos emerge from the fog, seven feet tall and magnificent, carrying a staff of gnarled wood. He walked slowly and calmly alongside the enormous length of the table, not once taking his eyes off the faerie queen. The queen also could not look away, although unlike the forest god's calm and liquid eyes, hers were frozen wide open in abject terror.

He came close enough to touch, then hovered over her. "Queen of Elfhame, you have broken our pact. You have deceived and cheated me and now you must be punished." He said this with tones one would use to a naughty but loved child.

Such was everyone's attention locked on the horned god that they did not notice Wyn follow behind him. She spoke, "this queen, my mother, has committed an act of treason. It was she who caused the death of our king."

Instantly a chorus of murmur's came from the crowd.

The queen turned to the crowd and said, "It was he who committed treason! He consorted with a human female and fouled our land by allowing humans to establish themselves. I saved Elfhame!" The nervous and defensive tones in her voice only succeeded in sealing her guilt in the minds of the attendants.

"She murdered the king and created this terrible bargain with the horned one which caused the destruction of the human castle, and the tithe we have paid lo these many years."

Angry and shocked mutterings came from the crowd like a chorus of crickets.

Cernunnos held out his hand. The hall became silent once more. For several agonizing moments the queen sat there, transfixed. Then, finally, she gracefully rose from her seat and allowed the forest god to lead her down the hall.

"Mother!" Morris exclaimed first and rushed to her, quickly followed by Nessa. Julia and Wyn stared at each other for an eternity, then Julia rushed over and joined the hug.

Dawns Maidens

Yule

Winter's icy wind whistled through the bare branches of the trees. In every home in Bunwych, ruby and sapphire logs glowed and popped in the fireplace. The inhabitants huddled around it warm in their bodies and hearts. Some sang songs, some told stories, some toasted bread over the fire, and some merely sat and watched the fire dance and sparkle. Millard and Bess' family were one such, and now that their true son Liam was home, looked forward to the winter solstice celebration starting in the morning.

In the newly restored parlor in the castle, Terrell and Lynneth sat together listening to Tomos, her father, recite a poem that Galvin had selected for the occasion. Galvin was there. Katrin was by the fire, roasting chestnuts.

Aldith and Alec were together in her cottage in the woods, doing what lovers do.

Wyn, although she was now the faerie queen and lived in the palace, missed her cozy cabin and brought the children there to sit by the fire once more. This time, however, Brogan was also there. With the power granted to her by the office of queen, she was able to break his curse once and for all.

Beltaine

Spring had finally begun in earnest. Bees impatiently bustled and buzzed their way into the not quite open cowslips in the shade of the hedgerows. The village green once again was strewn with countless garlands of flowers of many different hues. Once again Lyneth was there in her white gown but this time Terrell was by her side. They spoke the ceremonial words, and raised the loving cup; each holding one handle, and both drank from it, and they were now married.

Terrell had never, at least not yet, returned to the king. He signed a pact with Wyn, the faerie queen; she would allow her goblins to restore the castle and keep it and the town safe from the malevolent denizens of Elfhame, while he in turn promised to keep the town secret from the king and keep away marauding armies.

Wyn, along with her children, was present at the wedding and looked over and was pleased to see Liam and Julia holding hands. Alec now lived in Bunwych with Aldith, while Julia, Nessa, and Morris lived in Elfhame. Although Morris returned to Bunwych often when he was sick of faerie food, or to just have a splash in the river with his friends.

Galvin spent less time in his library and was observed frequently walking the town with Corliss, widow of the previous town baker.

About the Author

Jon lives in rural North Carolina in a 19th century farmhouse situated amidst pasture land and forest. His other hobbies are restoring historic properties, gardening, sculpting, and film making.

Please sign up for my mailing list. If you do I will send you a free short story.

https://jon-fabris-author.mailchimpsites.com/

If you enjoyed reading this novel, please leave a review on Amazon. I read every review and they help new readers discover my books.

Coming soon, a new novel by Jon Fabris, **Tales From the Age of Legends**

Made in United States
North Haven, CT
24 January 2023

31560760R00143